Cardiff
www.card

Llyfrge
www.caerdydd.gov.uk/llytrgelloe

Girl in Profile

ACC. No: 02658212

Also by this author

Seahorses are Real
Le Temps des Cerises

Forthcoming for children;
A Whisper of Horses

Girl in Profile

by

Zillah Bethell

HONNO MODERN FICTION

First published by Honno Press

'Ailsa Craig', Heol y Cawl, Dinas Powys, Wales, CF64 4AH

1 2 3 4 5 6 7 8 9 10

© Zillah Bethell, 2016

The right of Zillah Bethell to be identified as the author of this work has been asserted in accordance with the Copyright, Designs and Patents Act 1988. All rights reserved. No part of this book may be reproduced, stored in a retrieval system, or transmitted in any form or by any means, electronic, mechanical, photocopying, recording or otherwise without clearance from the Publishers.

ISBN 978-1-909983-41-0 paperback
978-1-909983-42-7 ebook

Published with the financial support of the Welsh Books Council.

Cover image: © Shutterstock
Cover design: Rhys Huws
Text design: Elaine Sharples
Printed by Gomer Press, Llandysul, Ceredigion SA44 4JL

For Loveday

For if we imagine this being of the individual as a larger or smaller room, it is obvious that most people come to know only one corner of their room, one spot near the window, one narrow strip on which they keep walking back and forth.

Rainer Maria Rilke

Art consists of limitation. The most beautiful part of every picture is the frame.

G. K. Chesterton

The progress of an artist is a continual self-sacrifice, a continual extinction of personality.

T. S. Eliot

Gwen

Beyond The Pale Of Myself

I creep along the edge of amethyst cliffs, palely certain he will come. My room is immaculate – only a hair of Edgar's out of place on the bed and a fish bone licked to China white (from Tenby of the Fishes I fled). He says to paint while I wait, but my jar of brushes remains on the mantelpiece beside the primroses just plucked. A work of art is a little beating heart, a little beating, palpitating heart, and I have no palpitations, no beats to spare, not while Rodin is alive. Though if I were to paint, I would paint this room, pretty and clean, awaiting his arrival – thrilling, expectant, anticipatory space. The lace curtains billowing, allowing the light to pick out each object – the barley sugar leg table, an open book, my hat and parasol, Edgar on the wicker chair perhaps – yet joining them all in one atmosphere. Mysterious, oblique. Time suspended, interrupted, me in the shadows, absent yet present. I hear his tread on the stairs. Quick. The lucky heathers peep, palely certain of the sun. The glass reflects an oval, that unruly strand of hair, the proud mouth still there, the cameo at my throat. We will enact *The Kiss*, I think, my skin a gleaming marble, my right leg over his lap. My wet clay. Sometimes he spits to moisten it. The delicate cathedral of his hands. I worship beneath.

Greetings next door. It is someone else. The sea mocks me with her cruel, cerulean smile. The sea is the very last thing to go dark. I'm almost tempted to throw myself in but I can do nothing. I should eat something. There is an egg, somewhere. If I get too thin I shan't be able to model for him. He likes his girls to be *dévelopée* (measured me with a compass the first time we met). Moonlight arrives with the fireflies and nightingales. I put on my nightdress and try to sing, but the noise of lovemaking through the walls is too loud. I am dumb like Hans Anderson's little mermaid (from Tenby of the Fishes I fled). Collecting cowries with my father and bluebells by the river Cleddau. Now he sits amidst mahogany and stuffed doves under glass, his foot firmly pressed on the sostenuto pedal of grief. My mother always a wave away from death – her life gone into her hats – travelling from one health spa to another for the rheumatism in her limbs. Augustus and I on the beach near Haverfordwest, drawing gulls and crabs in the sand and watching the neophytes plunge into baptism and then resurface, their selkie heads breaking the sea's caul in rebirth. As I am reborn in his hands. Prometheus. *Mon maître*. I lie between the sheets and do what only Rodin should. Edgar snores on top of the wardrobe. A cameo moon – goddess of invention – sieves her golden sand through the billowing lace curtains and onto the barley sugar leg table, the primroses just plucked, the egg gone cold. I lie awake and wait for the dawn, beyond the pale of Minerva, beyond the pale of myself.

Moth

Adam

He's wearing a white shirt and blue jeans, same as me. No visible tattoos. He's not the kind of guy to have a tattoo. Drew's got "Moth" on his chest and "Roan" and "Dove" on either wrist. Looks plain dirty if you ask me, and imagine when you're old. I drew the line, with a full stop at piercings. We're his heart and arms, he says. Load of crap. It's just his tribalistic, sadomasochistic, look-at-me way of displaying us. Branding. Establishing ownership rights. If you name it, you own it, isn't that how it works? Maybe that's why our rescue puppy doesn't come to command – we haven't named him yet. At the moment he's Treacle; only because he licked up a whole tin of golden syrup that fell out the cupboard when we were making Roan's school fête ginger cake.

His eyes are licking me up right this minute. I'm sugar-frosted all right. Cornflakes on my boyfriend jeans (and they really were my boyfriend's); snot from Dove's retroussé nose on my minging-as-Tracy-Emin's-bed grandad top (and it really was my grandad's); and an old-as-Stonehenge spunk stain (and it really was Drew's, whatever you may think) on

4

my pants – from the time we attempted to do the swamp thang in a ten-minute slot. (Lesson number one: don't attempt to do the swamp thang in a ten-minute slot when you're sex deprived, sleep deprived and think your children have just nodded off – they probably haven't. Creak creak thump thump and that's not the bedsprings, let me tell you, that's a little body climbing out, creeping across and suddenly appearing like frigging Caspar on the landing. Oh God, not now. Gearing up to full throttle. Mummee Daddee. Jesus Christ, get your kecks on, you'll scar him for life. Bad dream, honey? Why the fuck can't your mother have them overnight for a change instead of coming over here with sweets and violent computer games? No wonder he's having bad dreams. And come to think of it, why's it me has to remember her birthday when she's not even my mother, ditto sister, brother, Grandpa Jo, Aunty Jean and your Uncle Tobermory in Nairobi?) He's still licking over little old sugar-frosted me. (His retinas must be hypoglycaemic.) Pixie crop gone long and a body, well, a few more sit-ups and I'd be drop-dead beat.

Adam makes us sit on children's seats. (Lesson number two: if you're over twenty-five you won't be able to sit on a child's seat without looking like you've got haemorrhoids or worms. I've got both courtesy of childbirth, and a dog that eats snails and slugs out of molehills then unbeknownst to me licks my BLT.) There's a lump of brown clay in front of us – it looks like a massive dog shit – and we have to do something with it. A pooper scooper comes to mind, or one of those wonderfully environmentally friendly plastic bags people hang their dog shite up in trees in like Christmas baubles, so instead of stepping on dog shit you're more likely to have a bag of it fall on your head. Oh, happy days, sing the squirrels, scampering down the branch of a stately old oak, a bag of nuts. Before skidding to a stop. What the fuck? A bag of shit. Since when did dogs start climbing trees, crapping on our park bench?

A little girl sat next to us is glaring at her lump of clay. She's in the charge of her grandmother, who's glaring at a knitting pattern. "A fairy," I suggest and they turn to glare at me. I know how the knitting pattern and the lump of clay feel. Roan is already working on a stegosaurus. He's studying dinosaurs at school. He knows pretty much everything about them from the fastest (velociraptor) to the largest (diplodocus). A group on the far side of the room are painting the clay sculptures they made last week. A few girls are looking over at Roan (like mother like son). Even at eight he's got stars sketched all over him. I keep his dark hair short to show off the bones in his face – which are perfect – and his huge green eyes. (You can smell the grass being mown looking at those eyes.) Sometimes I wonder what Drew and I did to deserve such incredible kids. Our son, strong and clear as the daylight. Our daughter, deep and mysterious as an ocean.

"Black and white are tones," Adam says to the group on the far side of the room. "Repeat after me, black and white are tones not colours."

The parents look arty, sophisticated, pretentious. Brings out the rebel in me, to be honest. I start rolling up balls of dinosaur poop to go with Roan's steg. I wish I hadn't come, wish I'd gone to the shopping centre with Dove and Drew, picked out a tasteful card for his mother.

"Cool dinosaur." Adam snowdrifts over, pulls up a little chair between us. He smells of fireworks and clothes that have dried on a high washing line in a long thin garden at the back of a terraced house in a Swansea valley. Much like our own. I remember one winter Drew and I stood halfway up our washing line, the snow was so high and the air so quiet and still it was like the earth had wrapped its own heartbeat up in a scarf. We walked on top of muffled hedgerows and made angels on the roof of an Alfa Romeo.

"You could do a monster face, a dragon, a treasure chest."

"Ooh yes." Roan's the cat with the Cadbury's Cream Egg on his lap. He's forever collecting feathers and stones and little bits of rubbish in old shoeboxes. What is it with boxes? We live in them, are buried in them, keep our precious little things in them.

7

"That's settled then."

I flick my pixie crop gone wrong and caress the clay with my long delicate fingers. This is the way I'll caress your face, my fingers are telling him. Adulterous little piggies that want some roasty roast beef before they go to market. I'm hurtling towards death and middle age just being a mother, and in ten years' time a man like Adam won't be looking at me like his retinas need a double-shot espresso and glycogen boost. I'll be a bitter old horse pill by then, the sugar licked right off me. Lick me now for real, my fingers are screaming. His leg is six inches away from mine – still squirming courtesy of worms, haemorrhoids and a plastic orange child's seat. I want to cry, but Roan is beaming at me. This is fun. A magic box, a box that morphs into a dog, a boat, a collapsing toadstool.

"It needs reinforcing, see, at the corners." Adam smoothes over the cracks, strengthens the frail edges, covers holes with strips of clay. His hands are long and fine like mine. No wedding ring. I keep mine in a tiny box in a jewellery box in a drawer of my dressing table in a corner of my bedroom (like mother, like son). His fingers are curious, intense, teasing, tormenting. We're in bed already, there's no preamble, no date, no candlelight, nothing to say. We're making love in an art class under a naked bulb in front of my son and a bunch of pretentious still-life grapes. It's not decent, not civilised. What's wrong with me?

A woman wants to know if Adam could kindly take a look at the colour of her daughter's serpent, someone wants more clay, the little girl sat next to us is glaring at her grandmother's knitting pattern, her fairy still deep in dog shit. I'm in deep dog shit and I want to be seen. I want to cry and then be consoled by this man, this man I've never met before, the first man in creation. Transformed by him into something I've always been and never known. Until now.

Two days later the box hardens and goes brittle. Four days later a side falls off. Four and a half days later the rescue puppy licks it into oblivion. We're calling him Clay these days.

Elizabeth

Death Row

"Elizabeth, did you manage a log this morning?"

The swallows had flown from the eaves of Castle Banfi and the grapes were turning a slow vermilion. Chiara thought –

"Did you pass a motion this morning, Elizabeth? The doctor wants to know."

I can't hear you. I'm deaf, remember, and in any case I'm trying to read my book if it's not too much to ask. I don't have many pleasures left. It's about an old woman in Italy whose personal details have been deleted from the municipal database. She has officially ceased to exist. Don't I just know how she feels. Old and mouldy, losing my marbles apparently. Two left on the solitaire board. My eyes. Pick 'n' mix. Shit, pop, spit out the gumball machine. I've eaten them. Orange, blueberry, spinach.

"With difficulty." It's best to be honest.

Tinkerbell waves her magic wand like this and prescribes

melon for my pudding tonight and, if necessary, a firework laxative. "That should do the trick."

"The tits…" Peter Pan is wheeling away to the window in a thundercloud of Imperial Leather and last night's sardines. "The tits on those balls. I've never seen so many." Peter Pan is a dragonfly. At least he knows the language of dragonflies. And birds. And poems. Nurse Tinkerbell, for example, is a common darter and exhibits some seriously crepuscular behaviour. Like now for instance.

"Ten minutes, the Blue Room, we shall have the opportunity to write to some poor unfortunates on death row in America."

How ironic. Aren't we all dead already? They just ain't thrown the dirt on us yet. Look at me losing my whataretheyagain? Dragooned, euphemismed, metaphored in here by my own children (my son has three houses; you'd think I'd fit in one of them). What a view of Caldey Island and the sea. Yippee. And Wendy over there, photosynthesising in her chair. Wendy is a stephanotis. She was given a cutting from her dear friend Eleanor ten years ago and now she obscures her own light. I think I shall go back to my book if it's not too much to ask.

Chiara thought that the tragedy of old age was that at last one knew what to do with the youth one no longer had.

11

Oh, how poignant and true. I know what I'd be doing now if I weren't so fucking moribund. Constrained in every decade I've been. Stoned in my teens; pregnant and insecure in my twenties; husband, two children and a springer spaniel in my thirties; midlife crisis in my forties; age-defying creams and faradic machines in my fifties; and now in my sixties losing my marbles. Shit pop spit a cormorant pecked them out on the beach. What a view of Caldey Island and the sea. Lucky me. Where the monkeys live. They do a good chocolate fudge and ice cream. God, I wish Minnie would visit.

"Oh, my son." Peter Pan is twirling around in a cirrus of soap and sardine. "You should be on a bottle of cider, my son."

"What is it?"

"A green woodpecker."

"Oh." I told you he knew the language of birds.

Nurse Tinkerbell hands out the photographs. Mine is James C Smith number 1240668, Potosi Correctional Centre. Aged forty-two. Killed his girlfriend three years ago. Dear Lord. On his second appeal. Orange overalls, shaved head, very blue eyes. Like butter wouldn't sizzle. Wants to correspond with a woman between thirty and forty. I can do that. I remember it well. Still a stunner to be honest. 36, 24, 36 even after one husband, two children and that

12

dreadful Freckles. On the verge of an affair. Sometimes I wish I had, though my late husband was a dear—

James, I will write, *let us not talk of your crime. We've all done things in the heat of the moment and then regretted them or not done things in the heat of the moment and regretted that. Not that you shouldn't regret what you've done, of course…*

God, I wish Minnie would come. We could talk about her latest infatuation. Some Eton mess. Cream, meringue and strawberry cheeks. Lucky cow. Giving her kittens. That's what boys from Eton do, apparently. Give you kittens. My late husband never did anything like that. Only that wretched Freckles from the pound and two ungrateful children. (At least they flew, I suppose.)

Wendy has turned a conifer colour. "I shall make myself do it. I shall write to this poor unfortunate. Eleanor would have wanted it. That was the thing with Eleanor. She could get on with anyone: a criminal, a member of the aristocracy. She had the common touch, you see."

"Bunch of tits." Peter Pan has discarded his photograph and is wheeling away to the whatsitcalled. "Bunch of hoodies after fatballs, those tits."

Flew like arrows, my children. But my bow was too strong and they flew too far. Sometimes I wish I'd been a Maori in New Zealand with a couple of boomerangs. Then I'd know the language of butterflies. Then I know they'd come back.

Gwen

Rodin

Ma petite amie,
I am sincerely enrhumé, in bed with a steam kettle and beef
lozenge and that is why I could not keep our engagement. I
am saddened by your accusations. You must remember I am
very old, alas, and find it difficult to keep step with your
demands as well as my work. You can be quite immoderate
in your desires, dear Gwendolen, and I am an ancient vase
that will crumble if touched too much. (I should be kept in
a museum already with my own sculptures.) Try to rein
yourself in like the thoroughbred horses you English girls,
pardon, Welsh girls, race along the seashore, the cool breeze
turning your cheeks a violent hue. Be tranquil, be calm, I
implore you. Visit the bibliothèque, take a promenade, have
a bath in the rue d'Odessa, draw a picture of your cat in
charcoal with her tail straight up like a tree à Noël. And
remember to eat well – eggs are good for your constitution
as I have mentioned – your digestion will pay you later. I
will bring a basket of plums from the Villa des Brillants the
next time I come. Yours in tenderness, A.R.

14

Elizabeth

Autobahn

I am tired this morning and my stomach hurts a little as it always does these days. Too many marbles. Fuck pop squit. I'm dying of a very long and complicated word and I don't really mind apart from the grapefruit. Please let there be no grapefruit in the mornings. Just a nice cup of tea and a round of toast, like I had after giving birth. What a strain that was, despite the pethidine and the birthing pool Freckles nearly drowned in. What a life it's been, and now it nears its end and I don't really mind apart from the dying. Gurgle, gurgle, then it's curtains, Tinkerbell said. Not that my late husband gurgled much. Just went off on the autobahn. German word for motorway. Eight letters, two across. Found him stuck on the crossword. Never a linguist, poor man.

"Grapefruit, Elizabeth. Sugared segments just as you like it."

I can't hear you. I'm deaf, remember, and in any case, I'm trying to sleep, though the light is streaming from the fingers of those Caldey monks, stretching through my lace curtains and trying to tickle me under the chin as though butter wouldn't sizzle. Where's my book?

"Blue Room when you're ready. We have some replies from those poor unfortunates."

Ah, yes, our comrades on death row. Lots of waiting around still and trying to be civil. After you, my dear. Oh no, after you. (Peter Pan will be the first if he starves himself as he intends. One Brussels sprout a day now that he is "on the continent". He can't bear the smell or the embarrassment.) Just reading, sleeping, breathing, dying, in littler or larger rooms depending on your bank balance. (My son has thirty-three including his greenhouses. You'd think I'd fit in one of them. I could squash up next to an auricula if I had to.)

Tinkerbell hands out the letters. Wendy is visibly wilting. Mine is from James C Smith number 1240668. Ah yes, I remember.

Dear Elizabeth,

Hi, good to have the chance to know you. I'm not real good with words but will give it my best shot. If at any time you don't understand me or have questions, feel free to ask. I have little to hide and pride myself on my honesty and respect people for theirs.

I am a CP (capital punishment). I am forty-two years old, white, obviously a male. I killed my girlfriend. I am very upset and embarrassed by my actions. I have always had a drink problem which has helped me to fall short of most things, including being a father. I have two kids, Skyla and John. I adore my kids but, as fate would have it, I may never see them again. I have spoken to them a few times since I caught the case, but I don't speak with my ex-wife much.

I was raised in a poor family with little or no supervision. Mother worked her tail off to give me what I had. I am the eldest of two. My home town is north of Hannibal, Missouri (boyhood home of Mark Twain). About forty miles right on the muddy banks of the Mississippi river. I am a true river rat. A river rat is someone who lives or was raised on or around the rivers. Potosi is about seventy miles south of St Louis, about two hundred miles from home. I hope you're still with me.

My work history is very widespread. I've done everything from farming to trucking and most everything in between. I've done welding, mechanics, some electrician, pipe fitting, air conditioning and carpentered on occasions. Trucking is where I finished the last several years of my free life. I drove all forty-eight states and visited Canada as well. I pulled dry vans, tankers and flatbeds. The last years I pulled flatbeds and enjoyed it very much. I took life very

*serious and swore by the almighty dollar. I know now
that money can't buy happiness although it is a big help.
I was always afraid of not having money and now I
accept not having it.*

*We get rec six times a week, sometimes mornings,
sometimes afternoon. My house is an honour dorm so
to speak. Not mandatory, just our choice. Some days
when we have morning rec, I don't make it out because
I get up at 2.45 a.m. for work. We're normally done by
6.30, but rec's not till 8.30 so I get tired and go to bed.
I do make most rec though.*

*I prided myself on baseball. I'm a big Cardinals fan.
That's the legacy of my grandad. I also had a brother,
Maximilian, who jumped off the Golden Gate Bridge
when he was 22. I don't know why. I think God caught
him. I also like Westerns. You can't hide nothing in the
desert. Even the birds pick you clean. It's a land of truth
and revelation. I know now why Jesus was tested in the
wilderness.*

*You say you're a teacher and a dancer. Boy, that must
keep you busy. Next time, I need to think about it some,
and ask you more questions.*

May God bless you, James.

"Are you well, Elizabeth? You look pale."

18

Oh my weary pincushion eyes. I weep for this man and what he has done or not done and the choices we make and what is life after all but burping and hurting and above all waiting in littler or larger rooms. My daughter in her laboratory, chasing viruses. And here I am having to endure them. She says they look like flowers under the microscope. She knows the language of flowers and butterflies, my daughter, as well as viruses. *Viruses don't read notices.* I lost her somewhere magical, somewhere intellectual, like that Botticelli angel of a girl in *Picnic at Hanging Rock*. She never came back. And now my granddaughter in some Eton mess or other. Just hope she's not preggers. Preggers with kittens.

"He wants me to send pictures of my intimate bits," the stephanotis is stuttering. "Says I sound like a real horny bitch. Says that his cellmate points at his genitals in the shower and makes kissing noises with his mouth. Says if I send money he can get soups and sodas…"

Nurse Tinkerbell waves her magic wand like this and prescribes a teddy bear tranquilliser.

"Shall we go to lunch?" Peter Pan is all saddle soap and spicy Sardinia to disguise the smell of being "on the continent", but his feathers are warm. "For one Brussels sprout."

"Yes, thank you, Peter."

Gwen

An Eroticised Terrain

L'Homme Femme is wearing overalls and a coral necklace. No sitting in the ribs of a whale, no stays, no symbol of repression. She taps her ornamental watch – I am unpunctual – set by the clock at Montparnasse station. The room is a frozen stream and my heart echoes the stagnant cold. She will not light the stove. She will wait till I turn blue then make me do acrobatics – tuck, pike, straddle, star – to warm myself up again. At the end of the session, she will pad over on her pink puffy Pernod paws like a St Bernard dog and revive me in this alpine weariness. All for the sake of her rather mediocre painting: *Madonna in Repose*. I am a perfect Madonna with my oval face, my little hands and feet, my eternal smile of apology. Reined in like a thoroughbred. Gathered in like a fruitful harvest. Collected like a cowrie on the seashore where I trot my collected trot.

"Stop fidgeting." She cleans her brush in a glass of Pernod and studies me through lidless eyes. "You're thinner. Someone been eating you up?"

Rodin of course. Licked the organs clean out of my body.

Left the carcass, the bones. Femur, ulna, radius, pelvic socket. They swivel, gyrate, rotate on their own. Like the models Rodin uses who swivel, gyrate, rotate, reveal their sex to him, which he sketches frantically, not even looking at his paper. Little downy plums. A basketful of vulvas. Is that what he'll bring next time he comes? A basketful of vulvas? Rodent, I call him, when I'm angry with him – nimble eyes, bushy beard, up a drainpipe—

"Hold the pose."

That is an insult. I'm known for holding difficult poses. Look at *Whistler's Muse* – left foot on a high rock, head bowed, mouth open. And this isn't *Madonna in Repose*, this is *The Blue Madonna*, Madonna with Pins and Needles, Madonna doing tuck, pike, straddle, leapfrog. I wish she'd turn into a St Bernard dog and give me a glass of Pernod or something from one of those silver decanters, but she continues to labour with her paintbrush and I continue to earn my keep and think of Rodin. Is he thinking of me? Surely the strength of feeling in my heart must resound in some auricle, some ventricle of his. I followed him once to Meudon, the Villa des Brillants, saw his thorny Rose. Ah, sweet domesticity. She was old and dignified, and dignity, in the circumstances, was truly remarkable. His dogs. The pond. I sat in the grass and peeped as the field mice played the piccolo and crickets the woodwind, tapping out their songs on the branches of trees or rubbing their wings together. I think I saw his shadow in their austere dining room. Easy chairs are for the English, he is fond of remarking. Then I went home and I've never felt so lost and alone. Even Edgar and my room couldn't console me. I dreamed that night that we were on a boat, he and I, in some elemental region. The sea is the very last thing to go dark, he whispered to me. The sea is the very last thing to go dark.

Enfin, she has done something she is satisfied with, captured a little of the mysterious human form, managed to get beneath the fictional skin of pigment. I can rest. She has bought onion tartlets and beer from Les Deux Magots. I am delivered from this alpine weariness. We chew together.

"It is love, I suppose," she sighs through lidless eyes.

"Well, yes."

"It is always love in Paris. I came here to work in my atelier and produce great paintings, but I am surrounded by passion and distraction. The men next door share a prostitute every night for five francs. They told me. Even the air is sensual here, stiff with flower semen and the sound of insects mating. Filthy as a frying pan. Paris is an eroticised terrain. I see bodies all around but little soul. Do you think we can manage a bit of soul, Gwendolen Marie, in the next session?"

I doubt it. Not unless Rodin gets off his sickbed and

carries it here in his pocket next to his copy of *The Divine Comedy* – or in his outstretched hands. Doesn't let it slip between his hummingbird fingers, doesn't peck it to death.

Moth

Swallows

The phone rings. It's Adam. The fingers didn't lie, after all. Adulterous little piggies about to stuff down some roasty roast beef if they're lucky. I put on my husky-dog three-pack-a-day prince-in-the-throat just-got-a-cold voice.

"Oh, hi, Adam." Like I'm surprised. Not.

Drew, who is combing Dove's hair on the sofa, laughs. Wanker.

"There's been a cancellation, so if Roan wants to come to art club today…"

"Ooh, yes, he'd love to, wouldn't you, Roan?" Roan, who is reading a *Star Wars* comic, nods vaguely. Drew shakes his head vigorously. "But I'm not sure if we can."

"It doesn't matter if you're late."

He *sooo* wants me. I can see his voice travelling down the telephone wires in a sparrowful of sound waves. I'm wide open like a half-formed letter *o*.

"Roan *loved* making the treasure chest the other day."

"Yes."

Drew sniggers, and I look at the stain on the windowsill

24

where the treasure chest sat for two hours at most. On the pavement opposite, Hellboy from number 5 is polishing his mother's brass door knocker, which he does at exactly the same time every day. He's forty-five years old. One day I saw him screaming in his car like a freakin' psycho. The sound waves looked like motherfucking bullets.

"The class goes on till four so it doesn't really matter what time you turn up."

"Oh, okay." We're making love on a telephone wire in full view of the sky. If one of us touches the ground we'll both get fried. I raise my feet an inch from the carpet and try not to see Drew shaking his head, violently now. He's spent all week trying to illuminate some godforsaken Miss-Havisham -detritus-of-a-life attic, filled with boxes of china teapots, photograph frames and school reports circa 1940, and he wants to stand upright, get some fresh air and exercise. On a day like this. With Yoda. *I know.* "Oh dear, I don't think we can make it today." My wing touches a particle of dust. Yeeoow.

"Sure. Maybe next time." Sound waves curl into italics, a sparrowful of ashes.

I take my place on the red chair we bought in an Ikea sale, which doesn't match the blue sofa we bought in a different Ikea sale. "He said it didn't matter if we're late."

25

"Yeah, but still."

"I could have taken Roan on my own."

Drew laughs for the third time in five minutes. "No, you couldn't. You'd never find the way."

And there it is. The unadulterated, very unadulterous, truth. Even if I wanted an affair, Drew would have to mastermind the whole thing from Googling the rendezvous to pronouncing on my outfit to plucking the hairs from my chinny-chin-chin, to pruning my bush into a pleasing topiary. I'm stuck in this marriage like a lump of toffee in his teeth. Which reminds me…

"Did you use xylitol instead of sugar in their cookies?"

"Yes."

"And did you put the sunflower seeds in and the spirulina and granular lecithin?"

"Yes."

I read library books on the subject of children's nutrition. I know all about the good stuff to protect against the bad stuff.

"Darth Maul's got a red lightsaber." Roan looks up from his comic and his eyes remind me that we need to mow the lawn. "What does RRP 20.99 mean?"

"Has he? Oh, good. Drew, you need to mow the lawn."

"No idea, son." Winking at me.

I even hide vegetables in tomato sauce à la Annabel

Karmel, make spinach pancakes, blueberry smoothies, tangerine sorbets, sprinkle ground almonds onto breakfast cereals. When it comes to the kids I'm head of this little corporation. And it's lonely at the top, sometimes, I can tell you. I can't even delegate without checking all the minutiae because Drew would forget his cock if it didn't have a mind of its own.

"Yoda's got monkey."

"Drop it. Now."

"Shit."

I don't even let them drink carbonated water because those little air bubbles erode tooth enamel, and Wales has the worst rate of tooth decay in the whole of the UK. Dulcie from number 5 is beckoning Hellboy in. I've never seen such massive hands on a woman. She must have given Hellboy's dad an inferiority complex when she wanked him off. "In you go, Mel. Your tea's on the brew and it's coming to rain."

(Lesson number three. Do not be a toffee-sucking mother. Do not steal your kids' teeth enamel. Let them fly high over the telephone wires in a transcendental arc. Let them fly to Africa if they have to. However hard it is to let them go, let them go. Like swallows.)

"YODA. DROP MONKEY."

Yoda, as we're calling the rescue puppy these days, simply because he did a massive green shit after eating two green

27

felt-tip pens and his ears are starting to stick out at the oddest of isosceles triangle angles, is hightail-arseing round the room with Drew, Dove and Roan in luke-sky-warm pursuit. What kind of sick genetic mix is this? I ask myself. Collie humping spaniel humping setter humping Yoda humping dachshund humping poodle humping Jar Jar Binks. Monkey waves a felt paw from the jaws of a Cheshire cat grin and I watch Hellboy go back in, his shoulders sloping under the dead fucking weight of it all, the dead wait of it all, the love. I press my fingers to the pane and leave a perfect set of prints. I was here. I did it all. Guilty of everything. My breath creates a fully formed *o*, closed and sealed as clumsily as the body seals two frayed nerve endings without bothering to reconnect them first. Paralysed. Vicious. Round and round on the Circle line like the man who lost his job and went round and round on the Circle line until he met his wife going round and round herself. A line from a poem comes into my head – Louis MacNeice's "Snow". *There is more than glass between the snow and the huge roses.* More than glass, yes, and if you tried to walk through glass you'd cut yourself to pink ballet ribbons. There'd be mopping up, bandages, collateral damage. And you'd never find the last few splinters of glass. They'd lodge in the carpet, on top of dust jackets ready to strike – icicle bright and snow-queen deep – like the scalpels that stab

28

microlesions into the hearts and eyes of laboratory rats. Oh God, do you vivisect us all for the greater good? Prevent some disease in the stars and the galaxies? Is that the plan?

I get up, go into the kitchen, start the washing-up.

Elizabeth

Orgasms/Fairy Knickers/ The Language of Death

Peter Pan's wheelchair leans like a nonchalant bike against the rotten fence surrounding the ornamental pond. He's stuffing the bird feeder with the bread roll he pocketed at lunch. Yes, High View House has an ornamental pond – it's in the brochure – with two resident goldfish. I've only fathomed one.

Blue Grass by Elizabeth Arden. On the wrists, behind the ears. The stephanotis approaches, divining her way forward with her stick. We sink into the bench bequeathed by a relative of someone who sat and sank. Soon the earth will envelop us, liquefy our hearts until, tired of her embraces, we will pop out somewhere else like a ghostly snowdrop or brittle laugh. I've wet myself again just thinking about laughing and the other orifice feels uncomfortably damp. I do ten Kegels – this is worse than post-partum – and thank heaven for plastic knickers. Headwear, footwear, underwear is my motto, though I no longer support the upper balcony. It lolls against my ribcage like my brain lolls in my skull,

30

like students loll on the grass (though I'm quite sure my daughter never did, even at Cambridge), like Freckles' tongue used to loll out the side of his mouth. Better without, Tinkerbell says, in case of an emergency. What kind of emergency, I wonder? I was brought up to have clean underwear in case of an emergency, not no underwear at all. I have considered faking an emergency, however, faking an attack. Then they would have to visit. Well, I faked orgasms for forty years, there can't be much difference. *Ow ow ow.*

"Not since Jerry Song broke it off with me," the stepahanotis is whispering, "have I been so insulted."

"Who?"

"The love of my life."

"Oh."

"Eleanor said I was too fragile, though."

"Broad-bodied chaser." Peter Pan, all gravy and gravitas at lunch, is strangely ebullient now. It must be the lack of food. He's stalking a dragonfly with his binoculars. "Like a gigantic wasp. Copulation brief, mid-air." He wants to know what the sausages were like. All gravy and gravitas, I tell him. He sighs. "In comics, the little boy always drooled over bangers sticking out of mash in those thought balloons."

Satie is coming from the Blue Room. Three *Gymnopédies*. Sad, faltering, slow. How ironic. We sit in the sun yet still feel cold, and our dreams are old and diaphanous as a fairy's wing. Blue-veined. I can hear the tick-tock of Wendy's heart. Sad, faltering, slow. If the music were fast and furious we might just stand a chance.

Dear James, I will scribble. *I was Coppélia last night. I soared, the crowd roared. But let me tell you, training to become a ballerina is not inconsequential. There is sweat, sweat and more sweat. Strains, breaks, agony, tears beneath the perfect veneer, the polished show. Imagine a swan gliding on the surface of a pond and then think of the little webbed feet paddling beneath. The unknown depths, the reeds, the water snakes, the snares. Paddling for dear life, just to glide. Is it worth it for that moment of soaring?*

"Eleanor warned him off." Wendy's in the light but still in the shade. "Of course she knew best."

Too fragile, yes. We are all too fragile for what life has in store. Too diaphanous by half. Look at Peter Pan over there nibbling at some fungus growing from the rotten fence surrounding the ornamental pond where one widowed goldfish still lives. Fungus that looks like a pair of frilly knickers. He's chowing down on frilly knickers, the dirty bugger, like Freckles used to lick and slurp his own balls. He must be famished.

I wonder what will grow on me when I am in the ground. Who will drool into my bangers and mash, my old and hairy minge? Down there. Down there. I need to learn the language of death. Is it diaphanous as a bat's wing, fairy knickers, a vowel through which our soul has fled? Multiple *o*'s. *O, o, o.*

Gwen

Ordinary Colours

He sends a basket of plums instead of himself, with a note on how to cook them: boil with sugar and a liquorice stick. *They will exude a syrup.* I'm sure they will. I've eaten three with custard and Edgar has licked a couple, his *cinabre* green eyes blazing like an apple tree fire in the Preseli mountains, the Garden of Eden. Does thorny Rose know she grows a vulva tree next to his dogs, the pond? I am reading *Pamela* from the library and *The Idiot* by Dostoevsky. I have even copied out a quote from Balzac for him: "*qui voit la fleur, doit voir le soleil*". Improving myself for him. Muscling up in the shadows so that I can be strong in the light with him. Biceps, triceps, gluteus maximus. If I can see the flowers, I must be able to see the sun. Ida has run up an outfit for me on her machine. Crimson faille. When I wear it, the men in the street will shout out "*jolie fille, belle femme*" because I am. Ida is expecting her fifth, alas. My brother is a satyr. Thank God my children with Rodin are made out of bronze, marble and stone. Dreams of stone. *Je suis belle, ô mortels! comme un rêve de pierre.* Stone is immortal. It doesn't die.

I sketch myself in the mirror, sketching, representing myself as an artist (not a model or a muse), though I am barely there, a mere outline. You could stick your hand through me and tap Edgar Quinet on the head. I am absorbed into my surroundings, part of the grime, woodworm, molecules, dust. Is there a space beneath the surface of things for me to inhabit? How to find the colours ordinary life wears yet infuse them with the radiance and longing of memory, dream, desire? The green tea I poured for you from my ordinary teapot; the table we made no ordinary love on; the curtains we drew back to watch the ordinary starlight... What happened to me that I would happily darn his socks for him? What happened to the girl at Slade who drew the discobolus with tomato-coloured chalk, who cycled miles for the first daffodils? A strange little animal, they said of me there, addicted to violets and a little way of saying "oh dear" all the time, an emotion spontaneously voiced yet curbed. Passion and restraint at war within me. I wore black to emphasise my fragility, my neat little hands and—

Mon Maître,
My hands are in perfect condition, I can assure you, if
you want to finish Whistler's Muse. *You cannot leave*
her without any arms. Thank you for the plums, which

were delicious, though I would have eaten you with more relish. Please come. My body longs to be fevered, maddened, exalted with yours once more. I have cancelled all my engagements next week so you are free to visit whenever you wish. I have a new outfit to show you. I shall wait in my room, and if you do not come I shall wait at the station. My outfit is red so you shan't miss me this time. A man followed me the other day in the street, leering at me and, I think, trying to unbutton himself. I threw a tin of pâté at him, which made me angry afterwards because it was Edgar's supper. I am reading Pamela, *your favourite book, and I have some ideas on painting I want to discuss. How to represent the magic, the personality of ordinary objects as the symbolist poets aspire to do.*

With impatience,

your Gwendolen Marie.

God help me that I would happily darn his socks for him; allow my heart to dangle like a raindrop in his necklace of webs; be a mote of dust in his beam of light. Instead of my own.

Elizabeth

Sweating

You're the hyacinth girl, Peter Pan said when he saw all the flowers in my room. I used to fake orgasms for them. Flowers galorey my husband would bring the morning after, I can tell you. They look like viruses under the microscope according to my daughter. She's at the cutting edge of her profession, as is my son. They were too busy to come even though I nearly died. Let's hope the cuts don't run too deep. There's a letter from him somewhere I believe. Ah, yes.

Dear Elizabeth… (since when did he start calling me that?) *Boy, you lead an exciting life.* Oh, keep telling yourself that, my lad, if it makes you feel any better about shoving your mother out of sight, out of her poor old mind. *I've gotten a little stir-crazy the last few days as we've had lockdown due to the weather.* Ah, yes, I presume they cannot film when the weather is inclement as it often is in the remote areas my son ventures into – all for the sake of a language. He braves mistrals, monsoons, tornadoes and typhoons in order to record the last living dialects. "A language should be allowed to expire or expand on its own." I wish he showed me the same compassion. I'm just a bunch of words after all: old, still beautiful, dying (like Egypt in *Antony and Cleopatra*). I should be allowed to expire or expand on my own. Look at Peter Pan over there expiring at the rate of a bar of pubic hair-knotted soap, and everyone conspicuously fails to notice, whereas I fake an attack and all hell breaks wind. Sulphurously unjust if you ask me.

Talking of sweat, I like to sweat as it sure makes me feel like I've accomplished something. I went to rec today. I did my dips, a hundred to be exact, and ran a mile and a half, so my total walking and running came to nine miles. I used all of the two hours and forty minutes we got today. My ankles are sore, but I feel good about what I accomplished. I guess I should explain the dips I do. The dip bar is poured in concrete with two handles four to five feet off the ground. It then has two handles similar to a bicycle's handle bars coming out. You lower your body down and raise back up, it works the shoulders, back, chest and backs of your arms real good. I try to do them every day I go out. Softball days I normally skip them. I weigh about 225 to 228 now, and with that much weight I feel I do real well. I feel good about them, so I guess that's what counts.

We had some young Christian kids, aged I'd say 14

to 16, come in the prison on our side of the camp and plant flowers.

Wherever has he got to now? Potosi Correctional Centre? Dear lord. Whatever kind of language do they speak in there? Oh, I see, it's from James... Silly me.

I think they did a fine job and the colours kind of put a bright spot in my day. Most of the guys couldn't care less, but I look them over from about twenty to thirty feet away every day. I miss a lot of the stuff from the streets, some things as small as trees and good grass all the way to food and such. I always liked working in the flowers and garden and even mowing the grass, things people take for granted in the outside world. Sometimes it rains on our rec period and I just stay out in it because it's refreshing to me.

The movie, The Natural, *is a pretty decent movie. It'll kind of show you the game of baseball.*

Whyever would I want to know about that? Just like my husband, harpooning on about some film or other when I'm trying to do the washing-up. Feigning an interest in his interests. Feigning an interest in his cock. My mouth had to feign an interest, my hands had to feign an interest, my frou-

frou had to feign an interest, and it was flowers galorey the morning after, I can tell you.

Most movies about baseball make home runs out to be the whole game. Baseball is a great game, but there's so much more to it than home runs. Some of the game's greatest hitters like Roger Hornsby and Pete Rose made a living off of singles and doubles. Pete Rose got his nickname by the way he played the game. Charlie Hustle. Everything he did he did wide open, running bases and playing defence. Never slowed down, just pushed himself to the limit all the time. In my eyes, Pete Rose was and is the greatest player of the game of baseball. He's the all time hits leader. If you ever get to the US, do catch a baseball game, they're fun.

The 24th of July marked the 3rd year anniversary of my case. It seems so long ago. I took so many things for granted in the free world. People out there should be happy to mow the grass, wash and wax the car, do their own laundry and wash dishes in a real sink and not a little wash basin like we have. Like I say, it's amazing how nice I had it out there. I'm also an alcoholic and it was involved in my case. I thought I needed it to get through the day when I wasn't trucking. Please believe me I never drank when driving the tractor trailer, but

I sure as hell did when I wasn't. I, my friend, was a fool. It clouded my judgement, and together with depression I allowed it to ruin my life. I'm so sorry for all the wrongs I did. If nothing else comes of my case, I hope I can detour some kid from a life of crime and wrongdoings.

Like I preach to my aunt up in Quincy, Illinois, you need to enjoy life and live it to the fullest. Travel, do picnics or just go fishing. Do all the fun things you ever wanted. Tomorrow has no guarantees. You're in my prayers and in my heart. Oh, and Elizabeth.

Yes, my dear?

You don't know how much I'd like to see you dance.

Oh, James, they threw hyacinths, littering the stage floor like confetti. I sit at my dressing table – *en déshabillé* – tubes and tubes of kohl and mascara. It's the devil's own job to get off, I can tell you. I use Ponds cold cream and a flannel. Pots and pots of hyacinths. Flowers galore my boyfriend would bring the morning after a night's performance. You are the hyacinth girl, they shout from the stage door. (I have a persistently stubborn admirer. "You are the hyacinth girl, Coppelia," he shouts.)

41

Gwen

Gates of Hell

I hang with aching fingers over the precipice of rejection.
You have lumbago, you say. Lumbago, is it? Halfway up a
ladder in your white smock working on your *Gates of Hell*.
I'm at the gates of hell, a disembodied fragment yelling
frenziedly, repeatedly, but you don't deign to hear me. I love
you, damn you Auguste Rodin, you and your *Gates of Hell*.
I can smell your beard trimmed, singed and lavender-
scented through the open window, vying with the coconut
of the gorse and the rabbit droppings I stand on tiptoe to
avoid. (Imagine the nuns of the Sacred Heart creeping to
their early morning devotions over bead upon bead of rosary
rabbit droppings, sleeping dandelions and buttercups, and
now it is the Hotel Biron – a banquet of balls and bare
buttocks.) It is dusk. It is always dusk. My shadow fled three
hours ago at least (back to Tenby of the Fishes I'll bet). I've
only ever seen you at dusk, heading for the Gare des
Invalides, back to thorny Rose and sweet domesticity; or in
the candlelight of your studio when we "collaborated" on
the floor and you pinned a note to the door that said

Monsieur Rodin is visiting cathedrals. If I see that note tonight I shall surely slip, my fingers leaving an indelible print on the edge of the precipice. Rilke, your secretary, holds the ladder secure. Rilke obsessed with virginity, Rilke obsessed with death. Rilke the solitary beholding the mysteries through his lunettes. Oh, you men. You keep your wives, mistresses and children in separate little rooms in your head where we pace and wait, pace and wait, scuffing up the floorboards, dirtying the wainscot while you continue to work and create. I should like to see you at dawn. Every dawn. Do you grope a soft dough moon in sleep with your large thick peasant hands; chisel through the marble of night with your nose; drag birdsong through the eyelets of stars; hew at dawn with your glacial ice-pick eyes?

You have clay on your hands. I am here to remind you you have clay on your hands. Your white smock is streaked with it. Rilke brings soap and a basin for you to wash, cleanse yourself of all clay, his lunettes glancing like half-open windows for all the little rooms in his head. (Can his wife see out of them? Can his daughter see out of them? Do they get a little air to breathe or are they caught in perennial twilight like autumn moths half-suffocating in velvet curtains?) You turn to face me at last. Can you see through a glass darkly one of your unfinished sculptures – a tiny figurine you made at top speed, in between your ongoing

43

projects, keeping your hands and eyes nimble on me. I wave repeatedly, frenziedly, but you don't deign to see me. You step down, I step further *en pointe* in order to see, throwing out my arms to balance. All is assembled on the trestle table before you: dressing gown, tobacco, glass of milk. The door to your private studio opens then closes and a note is pinned that reads *Monsieur Rodin is visiting cathedrals*. I'm about to enter the underworld. I'm about to make my journey through hell. There are no devils at the door, only you in the clouds – the thinker – presiding over the whole affair. Why couldn't you leave me sleeping in marble? Why did you ever take a chisel to me? I walk around, ill-fitting my own skin, unable to produce my own shadow when I need to (back to Tenby of the Fishes it fled). It roves around the fishing smacks beached on the South Sands – *Periwinkle, Romany Lass, Cadwallader* – before curling up in the prow of the *Oyster Shell* like a dirty old tramp. Rilke shrouds your *Gates of Hell* with a large white sheet, keeping it warm and wet for next time. Who is she? Who can it be? Will you love her into a lunatic too? The way you loved Camille Claudel, the way you loved me? My life goes over the precipice, out of sight, out of mind. Rilke pulls the wooden shutters across, a lunette peeping like a delicate crescent moon. (Do they have a telescope in their room? Do they get a look at the Sea of Tranquillity, the Sea of Cold, the Sea of Crises, orient their

44

movements by Syrius the dog star, the Archer?) My shadow wakes in the grit of the *Oyster Shell*, rises with the pearly surf and the seagulls, cold, hungry, dry as old whitebait.

Moth

Bounce and Rhyme

I walk Roan to school, half dragging, half carrying Dove along too. Past the cinema seat cemetery (all munching their popcorn as our trailer trails by), past Mr Chan's takeaway still smelling of prawn crackers and crispy duck. I'm hungry, wails Dove, and I tell her off for messing about with some badge that says "I am three" on it instead of eating her breakfast. Past the new estate going up ninety-nine to the dozen. How fragile their infrastructures are. How precarious.

"Will Daddy put the lights on in them?"

"Maybe. If he gets the contract."

We see a white van in the distance and lay bets as to whether it's Drew or not. Dove shakes her dandelion hair and the seed thoughts disseminate, take root, spring up somewhere. "It's a different man in a little white van." How clever she is.

Over the disused railway track where coal-black cats with smouldering eyes bask between the girders, as if they've been tossed off a wagon on its way from the opencast mine that once sparked the valley.

"Jonah's here."

Ah, yes. Jonah's grandmother is reversing her black Skoda into a spot on the corner by Ebenezer's beds. We wait for them to catch up. Jonah might as well be stuck in a friggin' whale, he takes so long to get out of the car. We pant up the hill together, Jonah telling Roan about a computer character you can plug in like some kind of air freshener, and Roan, who's barely played a computer game in his life, nods wisely.

"I'm thinking of giving it a go with the new fella," Jonah's grandmother confides. In two years of panting up a hill together I still don't know her Christian name. "Moving in with him."

"Oh, well done you."

"Well done you," Dove parrots on my shoulder, irritatingly.

"You're a little cough drop, aren't you. Trouble is, I don't know what to do with Woody."

Woody is Jonah's grandmother's late husband.

"I'm thinking of putting him in my son's garden till I see how things pan out."

"Why can't he stay where he is?"

"I'm letting out the dormer for the summer."

"Oh, well, he'll be safe in your son's garden won't he?"

"I just don't want him getting knocked over and flying about all over the shop."

I try not to laugh at the thought of ashes from a purple urn disseminating, taking root, springing up somewhere like Dove's dandelion seed hair.

I affect a cool calm nonchalance at the school gates. I always have. None of the goo-goo Lady Ga-Ga stuff the working mums go in for, leaving lipsticked imprints on their children's cheeks before leaping back into their massive jeeps because, let's face it, they have to cross some mountainous terrain before reaching their offices ten minutes away. Most of the mums round here go back to work and the grandparents take over the childcare. The only other full-time mum I know is in hospital with a brain tumour. Doesn't that tell you everything you need to know about full-time isolating parenting? I never really had a job to go back to. Miss Carmarthen at twenty-two didn't leave me many career options except getting laid by the best-looking sparkie in town, which happened to be Drew, then getting pregnant, then getting married. I pat Roan on the head like he's the rescue dog, and he shines back at me. Those teachers' hearts must fill with fucking joy when they see him coming. God polished him before he came out. Polished till he saw his own face in him.

"You coming?" Fair play to Jonah's grandmother, she does try to include me in the geriatric small talk of the playground, especially since Maggie got her brain tumour;

48

but I draw the line with a full stop at an octogenarian zumba class.

"We're off to the library," I explain. "Bounce and Rhyme."

Rhys' grandad limps over on his zebra stick. How he keeps up with that little fucker Rhys, God only knows. He's a bit of an old perv, Rhys' grandad, but he's nice enough. He's got the oddest way of licking his lips when he speaks, which Dove invariably tries to imitate. The effect is beyond rude.

"You won't know what to do with yourself when the – *lick lick* – littlun goes to school."

Dove *lick licks* back at him, her eyes as innocent as china-blue plates.

"I'm sure I'll think of something." Like having a shit in peace, having a cup of tea in peace, thinking for a microsecond in peace without a child chirruping in my ear like friggin' Tweety Pie.

We trudge down the hill at a snail-in-its-shell pace because everything in the world is a mystery to Dove: the worm on the pavement, a lemonade can, some crazy old lava lamp in a window, a lion door knocker. I put on my breathless excitable voice as if I'm seeing the objects for the first time too. Drew thinks it's weird, but it comes natural to me. To be honest, everything with kids came natural to me. I had perfect pregnancies, perfect births. I didn't even get a single stretch mark. My friends have stomachs that look like road maps left out in the rain and they want to know my secret. Well, here it is, *The Six Million Dollar Man* top tip – pumpkin seeds. Eat a handful every day and you won't get stretch marks. As for the birth – keep active. Scream, shout, kick your partner in the goolies, push like you're doing a crap. Job done.

The library's bustling with old folks, all after the latest large print erotic thriller by the look of it. God almighty. How soon we grow old yet we don't really change. Still gagging for it, still looking at ourselves in the mirror. Our lives are like fish that slip through our own nets. We never seem to catch them. We sit by the river waiting for them to jump out at us. In the end all we get is an old boot, a clump of weeds. Oh to be wise and mature, having lived a life full of meaning, without regrets.

"Shall we start with 'Twinkle Twinkle'?" the librarian asks.

Why not, we always do. The grandparents start to croak. I start to croak. A young mum – I try to check my excitement – starts to sing. Actually sing. I look at her with suspicion. This can't be right. She can't be a full-time mum after all. She must be on maternity leave. Knowing it will all end soon she's loving every minute of it. Look at those hand gestures to "The Wheels on the Bus". Those aren't the hand gestures of a full-time mum, I can tell you. They're far too vigorous. My heart goes down on me like a dirty old man would if I let him – fast, rough, slobbering. My suspicions are confirmed when we stop for a tea break and she asks for a cup of hot water, no biscuit. Gracie's grandad and I exchange a look of pure bafflement. What kind of creation is this? He's bereft even of gardening tips. We've been up since the bum crack of dawn. We accept anything we're offered – antiseptic throat lozenge, chewing gum, cream cracker. Say the words 'chicken casserole with dumplings' and a full-time parent's liable to wet themselves.

"Is that some new trend?" Sydney's great-grandmother asks, shocked and shaky.

"Oh, no. I just want to feel like me again for when I go back to work. I'm a project manager, you see."

I see. My heart is a submarine. When did I ever feel like me? I dunk my digestive, Dove appropriates the librarian's mug even though it's got the librarian's name on it. There was a small power struggle for a couple of weeks which Dove eventually won. She usually does. She could bring a grown giant on stilts to his knees, that one. Gracie's grandad gives me some ideas on crocuses. Sydney nearly chokes on a deseeded, deskinned grape. A guy comes in with a trolley full of books. He stares at me just to add to my paper clip of stares. I'm a magnet for them to be honest. He's not bad looking. I imagine him taking me against the library wall –

51

hard, fast, intense. Then I think of Drew lying on the mat in the children's room so that he can comfort them easily when they wake from a nightmare. Guilt is eternal, not love. Dove and I choose a book about a girl with a magic paintbrush. Everything she paints becomes real. The keys to escape from jail, the horse to ride away on… Lucky fucker. We step out into the sunshine and I rally car myself for the journey home, which will involve many mysteries, distractions, detours…

"Listen to the birds, Mummy." Dove tilts a pixie ear to catch the birdsong.

How loud it is. Surprisingly loud. And persistent. Like the birds have had too much to drink and are getting shouty with each other. The young guy comes out of the library with an empty trolley and winks at me. So sure of himself. I flick my pixie crop – to match Dove's pixie ears – gone long and smile.

"What do you think they're singing about?" I ask her.

"Anything." Like I'm an idiot. "They're just happy."

How clever she is.

Elizabeth

Pathos and Bathos

Peter Pan sits on the wicker chair beside the window and reads to me. His profile against the ultramarine blue of the sea is pale and sharp as a cliff, and his hands hover like gulls about to swoop on a chip over the pages of *Crickets of Great Britain and Ireland*. He'll read anything he can lay his hands on, anything those gulls can snaffle from the mobile library each week. It's a substitute for eating. He gobbles syntax, devours the parts of speech, hoards metaphors under his pillow for when he gets the midnight munchies.

"The scaly cricket is wingless and therefore silent. They use their wings to sing, you see. Without wings there is no song."

I think of the wings I stitched laboriously for my daughter's ballet classes, my son's plays. The roots I dug, the wings I stitched so they might fly, so they might sing. Instead of me. Resentment swells up in me like a stale old fart. What did I do with my amazing beauty, my verve, my vitality? I gave them away to one husband, two children and a dog. And for what? The dog's long gone to a land of sniffs and smells, husband's raced off down the autobahn, and the children have flown so high and sung so loud they don't deign to see me anymore, they don't deign to hear me.

"We are merely groundhoppers. Eating liverwort."

I lobotomised my own life for them. Willingly. Eagerly even. That is the extraordinary thing. I wanted to do it. I stayed at home, kept my eyes on *kinder* and *kirche*, didn't take my chances, passed the open windows, ignored the innuendoes from the men who might have.

"When I was young..."

"You were never young, Peter. You were born immediately old like one of those peculiar lizards."

"Well, I was actually, as a matter of a fact. Once upon a time I was young, and when I was young I set more store by the apprehension of things than the things themselves. D'you know what I mean?"

I think I do. Like the alternative life I lived in my head complete with soundtrack, frantic sex, high-speed car chases, mysterious assignations, passionate illuminations... And now it is all constipation and colostomy bags and Satie coming from the Blue Room. Sad, faltering, slow. Like the tick-tock of Wendy's heart that beats like a metronome. When the music stops so will she. We don't stand a fucking chance, do we.

"Now I want to immerse myself in the things themselves.

Feel the thinginess of things, if you know what I mean. Sometimes I think it is a premonition of death when we dissolve into all things, into each particular thing."

"Hamburgers for lunch," Nurse Tinkerbell announces from the exit door.

Is that bathos or pathos? I'm not really sure, but the gulls wheel away, screeching, over the waves of Peter's hair, and the little book on crickets slides to the floor.

"Oh, and Elizabeth, you have a visitor."

My heart leapfrogs over all the other little children's hearts. It must be Minnie.

"Doctor Kharana wants a word."

A word. In the beginning was the word. What word will I end with? I need to learn the anagrams of life. Heart is an anagram of earth my late husband used to say. Never a linguist, poor man. Stumpy little tongue. Never a cunnilinguist either for that matter. The secret is to spell out the alphabet with your tongue. Most women have a favourite letter. Mine was *m* I seem to remember. The most curvaceous letter in the alphabet. Mmmm.

Gwen

Bousculé par le Monde

Dear Gwen Marie,
Your letters are very touching, ma cherie. If you are so
sad in your room you must change the apartment. I will
gladly send money for this. I have always thought your
atelier to be a little damp – damp enough for
champignons in my opinion and not good for someone
of your constitution. You must regain equilibrium of
mind and body. Immodesty is not charming in a
woman. Leave Paris for a while. Visit the countryside,
look at the flowers and the starlings. Take a deep breath
of nature and she will pay you later in blossom. I am
bousculé par le monde as always. I must curtail
everything in order to work. The promenade of one
evening and I am debauched. You, as an artist, can
understand that. Fundamentally I am a private man,
a silent man, like a great moon that looks over an
unknown empty sea where few ships pass. But I will
visit you again, one day soon.

Your affectionate friend, A.R.

The twice weekly trip to market, nightly bed, daily meal, midday cup of tea when the houses opposite cast great shadows like dirty old tramps peering in at me. Ida sends a concoction of honey and coriander for my throat – it is bad again – and Dorelia sends a silver brooch. They are in the south of France, bathing their children in sea water to cure them of freckles. Ida is square as a box and mad as a lemon squeezer, so she says. The baby is due soon, just to add to the collection. They pop out whole and splendid as dolphins, her boys, leaving her shrivelled as seaweed. My brother is a satyr. Does he sleep with Ida one week, Dorelia the next? Do they take alternate shifts in bed, creeping into the soft contours of the one that has left? Do all men need more than one woman to be happy?

One day soon. My heart tries to leap like a rabbit in the dilapidated gardens of the Hotel Biron, but I grab it by the neck with my tiny wee hands. Aha, little rabbit, you can strain, kick your legs, bulge the whites of your eyes at me, but I've got a good hold on you. Little darting heart that you are. He is *bousculé par le monde* as always. He is every e-acute you care to imagine: *enrhumé, bousculé, agité, âgé.* E-acute is a chronic condition with him. He is unrepentant, admits nothing. Am I to love flowers and cats for the rest of my life like a sad old spinster? Is that all I'm good for? I would not take a sou from him. I would rather wear my crimson faille through the winter, survive on one lump of coal a day, sit in a fairy ring of champignons with Edgar by my side. I shall work for L'Homme Femme, sit for her every day, maybe find a model of my own and put the energy of loving into drawing. I will paint her in this room, emaciated, etiolated by spiritual anguish and love, and I will present it to him with the words: *This is what you did to me, Monsieur Rodin, this is what you did to me.*

Elizabeth

Cuckoo's Nest

Doctor Kharana looks at me like butter wouldn't sizzle, but I know better, the randy bastard. Saw him pinching Nurse Tinkerbell's bottom in the corridor only this morning. They think I don't notice, they think I'm just a dot-to-dot old bint reading my book about Italy and the vineyard and the skeleton of the whale they've just found beneath the vines and poor old Chiara, whose husband is a philanderer. She's a common little darter, Nurse Tinkerbell; Peter Pan's read up on her in his dragonfly book. He knows the language of dragonflies. And crickets. And toadstools. My son is a globe skimmer apparently, and I'm a banded demoiselle – that's right, a banded demoiselle. I've lived most of my life underwater as a nympho from what I can gather.

"Are you happy here, Elizabeth, at High View House?"

Hell yes, wouldn't you be? Three meals a day, shit when I need to, stephanotis who's swallowed a clock, and an emaciated stink for company. Pen pal on death row for murdering his girlfriend, husband who fucked off down the autobahn just sitting in his chair, children who behave like

Icarus without the scorch marks and the downward descent, and a granddaughter in some old Etonian mess and a view of Caldey Island and the sea. Yippee. Lucky me. Lucky old effervescent-vitamin-C-to-perk-you-up-a-bit me.

"Do you get confused sometimes between what is real and what is not?"

Heavens, yes, of course I do. I don't even know where I lived my life. Was it out there in the streets and the suburbs, in the rain, in little rooms? Or was it here in the hippocampus of my head complete with safari tent and gear? Does it really matter anymore? My life still goes on like a television set, I take my KitKat tea breaks in the synapses of my brain.

"It's quite normal at your age to get confused, to have one or two aches and pains," he smiles, though his eyes are cold as Dairylea straight from the fridge, and even though it's spreadable it still rucks up the bread. "Now that you're in your twilight years."

Twilight, yes, when you can barely see or be seen. When you flit home from one lit window to the next until you reach your very own. When we're not quite light yet not quite dark, not quite lit yet not quite extinguished. Crepuscular, in fact, like Nurse Tinkerbell's face at the exit door as Doctor Kharana shakes his head and announces for the benefit of my twilight ears, "She hasn't said a word."

60

I shout suddenly, red and blustering as a bare-cheeked gale, "I'm fine, Doctor Kharana, absolutely fine. Why don't you check on Peter and his calorific intake instead. Have you seen him recently? He's shrivelled as a pea."

Nobody says a word. The birds outside are louder than us. They have a bit of song left in them. I slump, and guilt engulfs me with my pillow. Oh, to be smothered by Chief in *One Flew Over the Cuckoo's Nest*, to follow him out, out through the broken window, the open window, the hippo decamped for good.

Gwen

Rape

I paint Fenella in my room. She's vulnerable in the waning light like a fawn that lingers too long by the edge of the lake, like Leda half dreading, half anticipating her rape. I start with slow smudges of curl, delicate feathery strokes from mid-air, building up skin, pigment, flesh on canvas. Her shoulders are bare, sloping, angular. My paintbrush undresses her further, unties the black sash from about her waist, lets the pretty white Romany dress slip to her knees. I have to catch my breath as it runs away from my body. I curve a breast into place, reveal another, lick an areola star into being. She is pale and thin as a fairy grown by the light of fireflies. She was meant for the shadows. I lengthen her limbs, deepen her, take her to extremes. Her left hand curls in mild protest. I tauten a sinew in her neck like tuning a violin string. She flinches. I show the whites of her heavy, lidded eyes, force her to look at me directly as I look at her. Not a particle of her body escapes my gaze, my touch.

Her mouth opens in defiance. When will it be over? Soon, my dear, soon, I lie. I take my time over the torment in her face, the bewilderment, discomfort. My breath is shallow, hoarse as a dog on a chain. The world diminishes, contracts, becomes grey and meaningless. Only her body shines, enticing me, provoking me. I gouge a belly button, hollow a collarbone, shadow the inner side of her thigh. I scratch her irises out through pity then scratch them in before slitting her downy plum in half, until vermilion juices trickle down my wrist, my chin. She sobs. I've gone too far. I paint out quickly, cover the mess with the pretty white Romany dress, give her a pendant as a token of my regard. Her long neck droops under the weight of it. She's wilting out of the canvas, acquiescent at last. The light dies. She is mine. (She lingered too long by the side of the lake.) I take over where the light left off. I paint my desire into her, my frustration into her, the whole of my sick and debauched little soul into her. This is what I did to her, God help me, this is what I did to her. And this is what you did to me.

Moth

Women's Work

I lie in the bath water Roan and Dove have probably pissed in. Plastic toys bob around me and an orange duck laps between my legs like it's giving me oral sex. I allow myself to think of Adam.

"This dog's been rolling in fox shit." Drew is washing Mr Stinks, as we're calling him now, under the outside tap. "What the fuck's wrong with him."

BC (before children) I indulged in long luxuriant baths; I might listen to the radio, light a candle, dribble a little aromatherapy oil into the cascading waves. BC I conditioned my hair; BC I prepared honey, strawberry and egg yolk face packs to keep my Miss-Carmarthen-at-twenty-two skin radiating Miss-Carmarthen-at-twenty-two. BC I had beautiful feet. Now, ten years later, I lie tense and crouching in a leaking shower cap and a piss-filled bath waiting for Drew to finish cleaning the fox shit from Mr Stinks, come in, and sit on the toilet seat so that we can get a word in that is not edgeways round the head of a child, the washing up, the Monopoly board, the Wii.

Tom whistles in the bathroom next door then urinates: a steady stream, a pause, two drops, the flush, the light switch. All the bathrooms in this row are ground floor, flat-roofed extensions. All are cold, all are mouldy. Tom looks like a member of a boy band who's bedded his mate's mum. He and his girlfriend have a baby girl called Cherry and, what do you know, grandma lives the other side of us at the ready. She's a bit of a Rottweiler, but she sure sings some sweet lullabies as she wheels the kid up and down the bleach-fizzing pavement. Tom collects his lunch from her every day – a tin of beans on a plate. Don't ask me why a grown man gets his lunch off his nan every day – it's beyond my comprehension. They call each other cunt over our garden gate. It's some kind of endearment with them. "Hiya, cunt" like you might say "hiya, love". "Cherry's a little cunt, innit?" like you might say "Cherry's a little coughdrop," and, appreciatively, "Nan, you're a real cunt…" like you might say, "Nan, you're a real godsend." We're sandwiched between cunts. It can't get better than this, can it?

The night is youthful. Ten o'clock, the kids are asleep – this is babyless bliss – an hour of mindless TV and then bed. That's the plan. I add more hot, try and drive the minutiae out of my head. Roan needs a Fair Trade banana for tomorrow, there's that ridiculous Victorian homework, a clean cross-country vest for Saturday, the photo he wants to show Jonah because it's funny and he's eating an ice cream, dig Dove's scribble out of recycling because apparently it's a masterpiece of daddy in an aeroplane, and more fish oil for their IQs and Dove's skin. This stuff is women's work, I've noticed. Men deal in broad outlines, women fill in the minutiae.

Drew comes in, dips his fingers in the bath, so I'm swirling in fox shit as well as children's piss. Thank you, universe.

"D'you remember Ro's got to take a Fair Trade banana tomorrow for school?"

"You what?"

"You've just proved the point I've been making to myself. That without me this family would fall apart."

"You're a frigging marvel. I keep telling you."

"Are you being sarcastic?"

"No, not at all. There's another mess I've got to clean up on the step now, else I'll tread in it in the morning knowing my luck."

Off he goes to clean up all manner of shit: dog shit, fox shit, bullshit – he won't take any of that. He says it like it is, does Drew. He's a grafter, my mum said when I married him. A real grafter. In no way could you describe him as an intellectual. She breathed the word like it was something special: intellectual. I close my eyes and allow myself to think of Adam. There's a faint cry somewhere. I squeeze my eyes, hoping it's a bat, a fox, Cherry.

"Mummeee." It's not.

"DREW." The cries become more frantic. "Oh, for fuck's…" I heave-ho myself out, dripping, freezing, clutching a towel, stomping up to the children's room. Dove is sitting up in bed, her eyes gleaming in the frigging gloaming at me.

"What is it, Dove? What's the matter?"

"I'm thirsty." With an internal sigh I hand her the cup of water that sits next to her silver-painted horse on the bedside table. "I'd have thought that at three-and-a-half you could get your own water at night."

"Oh yes, but it's better when you get it… Mummy, you're all wet, like a mermaid."

"That's because I was in the bath. I was in the middle of having a bath, trying to get a bit of peace and quiet from you lot."

"Did you know," Roan announces from his bed, his star globe shining Cassiopeia at him, "that in the old days people used to stand on the roof and pee down on you."

"Good boy, go to sleep now."

I do the obligatory kisses on the heads, the tuckings in once more. I'm halfway to the door.

"Mummy, are goblins on this earth?"

67

"No, sweetheart. Just pretend, just in books."

"I thought I saw one. By the window."

"No, that's just your brother's Fair Trade mobile, remember, the one he made out of bottle tops."

"Oh."

I'm halfway through the door.

"Mummy." It's Roan's turn to pipe up again like a frigging Scottish reel. "Mr Sullivan gave me a gold certificate today."

"Oh, what was that for?"

"He found it under the table. He asked if anyone wanted it. I was desperate to get it."

"I see. Well, goodnight."

"Goodnight, Mummy."

I stomp down the stairs, stick my head out of the dog flap, and hiss at Drew. "When I'm in the bath, make sure you're inside, all right." Then I stand about morosely in the kitchen. There's no point going back in the bath now. My shower cap's still hanging on to my head as if it were Tom Cruise in *Mission Impossible*. The only thing that'll save me tonight, I mutter, is cheese and crackers. BC I didn't talk to myself or stuff down cheese and biscuits at ten o'clock at night with the last dill pickle in the jar. Or possibly I won't, seeing as how it's mouldy.

The phone rings. What fucking idiot phones at this hour?

"DREW… Oh, for fuck's…" I chew and spit some cheese

out as quickly as I can, run for the sitting room, tripping over some pink fluorescent took-two-hours-to-unwrap-and-will-probably-end-up-in-landfill plastic toy and answer the phone in the take-it-easy-Cadbury's-Caramel-rabbit voice my mum used to use on my dad sometimes. In case it's Adam. It's not. It's Steven, Maggie's husband. He's been looking after the kids since Maggie got her brain tumour. He gibbered so much at the doctor that he got six months full pay, six months half pay. He's way past that now and on statutory sick pay. He sounds like he's being strangled, which he probably is.

"Maggie's coming out next week."

"Oh, wonderful, Steve."

So could we look after the boys on Saturday so he can tidy up a bit.

Drew is suddenly behind me, gesticulating. Wildly. No. Absolutely not. Not in infinity years.

"Yes, of course, no problem. How is Maggie?"

"All right, I suppose. She's got no neck."

"What?"

"There's something wrong with her neck now. And she's got a limp."

"There are probably stretching exercises…"

"And don't forget Jamie's medication has to go in the fridge."

"I remember." Their eldest kid, Jamie, has got ADHD. They get given loads of money to send him on adventure holidays. He's been white-water rafting, abseiling and potholing, and he's still as mad as a rat. They even got money for a trampoline.

"If he does enough roly-polys," the key worker said, "he's not going to stab his little brother in the eye, is he?"

"It's very kind of you," Steven apparently replied, "but I'm not quite convinced of the logic of that."

I put the phone down, hum a little tune, avoid Drew's evil eye. I'm not just in his bad books, I'm in his Salman Rushdie books, as my mother would say. How soon we become our mum and our dad. He's not even doing the hundred skips, press-ups and v-sits he does every night before bed to keep his body looking ripped, cut and buff. They sound like characters from a western, don't they: ripped, cut and buff. There's only one thing for it – I get up, walk over, let the towel drop just to remind him what he's got. (Women's work again.) Then I go into the kitchen, make more cheese and crackers, put the last dill pickle on top, present it on a plate like the head of John the Baptist.

"Yum." Drew grins. Mr Stinks wags his tail. He's a passion for dill pickle, that dog.

It's all in the details, I'm telling you. The minutiae.

Elizabeth

Wishbones

Wendy's all sympathetic foliage. Sometimes I wish she was deciduous, I have to say.

"You did the right thing." She pats the air above my arm. If our bones should meet they'd surely break. Two pinkies could pull our legs apart like wishbones. "He was, after all, starving himself to death. It's what Eleanor would have done."

I bet. The meddling old witch.

"She always did the right thing, whatever the cost to herself, to others… They've been feeding him up on milk for premature babies, jelly beans, chicken broth, marrowbone."

I groan. Where's my book?

"I barely recognised him, spilling out of his wheelchair he was. A little *piano*, I suppose, as Eleanor would say. A little dishevelled. He said, 'Do I dare eat a peach, Wendy. Do I dare eat a peach?' And I said, 'Oh, do dare, Peter, do. It'll put roses in your cheeks.' His wife died of an eating disorder, apparently. All the good things he cooked for her she spewed back up in his face."

The print is blurry.

"Nurse said he could go on for years, now that he's eating properly."

Fucking cunt. It's all I am, all I ever have been. Please forgive me, Peter, if you can.

"Of course, one wonders how long one wants to go on for. Doesn't seem much point without Eleanor. All I have left of her is a few knick-knacks. Good of her to leave me anything really – after all, I'm not family. Just the dog's bowl, a fox print I once sent her."

"I thought she was very rich."

"Yes. Yes, she was."

I can hear the tick-tock of a melancholy heart. Sad, faltering, slow. Satie floats through from the Blue Room, pages turning in a restless mind. What is life after all but the tick-tock of melancholy hearts, pages turning in a restless mind. Hurly-burly, wind driven. I need to be forgiven.

Gwen

The Narrative Gone Elsewhere

I wake to find L'Homme Femme stroking my arm, checking me for goosebumps so she says. I've dozed off in the middle of another interminable sitting for *Madonna in Repose*. Like the tramps from my childhood who fell asleep on top of lime kilns, sank, were asphyxiated, ashes by morning.

She takes a gulp from the glass of Pernod she normally cleans her brushes in, hides her hieroglyph eyes.

"I would, actually," I tell her, "if Rodin wanted to watch. I've done it before." And I have. A spectator joined in once when we collaborated on the floor.

Her eyes betray nothing as she scrabbles in her dressing-up box for a hat and scarf. It is snowing outside. "I'm taking you to Les Deux Magots. I can't paint you this thin."

I yawn, get dressed, flaunting my modesty yet protecting it, gauche yet faux naïf, vulnerable yet omnipotent. Does she see what Rodin sees? All the ways in which a body aches against mortality. My belt is loose; I am too thin. My money goes on paints, canvases, outfits for Rodin to see me in, undress me in.

We step out into the snowflakes, each of them unique, each of them talented. And there are so many of them. I allow one to melt on the blue veins in my hand and think of my work, my painting, the empty canvases in my room. I run to escape the thought and L'Homme Femme lollops beside me in her purple velvet trousers, faithful as a dog.

Les Deux Magots is steaming with cocoa, aromatics and tobacco. I see him straightaway, in a corner of the room with a red-haired young woman. Henna or a wig. Sleek as a fox. The sort of woman I've tried to be for him. She places a finger on his lips as though delivering a kiss or stopping his speech. He's wearing a greatcoat, his hair and beard fizzily damp. He reminds me of Cadwallader, the giant from Tenby who strode silently through the town in oilskins, holding a shrimp net. All the little shrimps Rodin catches in his net.

"Cocoa and syllabub?" L'Homme Femme has to repeat it. I nod and cry – there is a snowflake in my eye. Pretending to look at the *jonque*, the second-hand goods on display. Books, pictures, old dolls, a musical box, a dandelion paperweight. Time suspended, interrupted, me in the shadows absent yet present. The ordinary girl. The invisible girl. Am I so absorbed into my surroundings that he doesn't even notice me?

Their profiles, giggling ivory cameos against the ochre-hued wall. The glass is smooth, heavy. It could hurt someone.

74

"There you are. Anything quaint?"

I point out the shrimp catcher and his trawl. "Imagine that wild gentian head between his knees. It'd probably come off the same time he does. Kiss me now, if you dare."

She does, vehemently, spilling the tray of cocoa and syllabub. Rodin notices as I intended. Gets up.

"You are part illusion." Her lidless eyes, the scalded arm accuse me.

"How's my starling?" The wet lapels of his coat, the thickening waist beneath, the hands that rub, smooth, caress new clay.

"Cold. Lonely. Miserable without you."

He peers fixedly at me. His eyes are the colour of the veins in my hand. What does he see? The ordinary girl? Can he distinguish me from my surroundings, the second-hand goods on display?

"Do you remember this body? How you used to say it was like the sun breaking through the clouds?"

"I remember."

"Promise then. Promise you'll visit soon."

"I promise." Hollow. Hollow as a tree where fairies dine, blow dandelion clocks. This paperweight could hurt someone if I let it. I imagine it splintering off his heavy skull, startling the henna-haired woman. Time released, recontinued.

I watch them all wave away. From now on I shall paint

pale women in pale rooms, their hands left holding the dead weight of some object: a book, a letter, the body of a cat. The story told. The narrative gone elsewhere.

Elizabeth

Augustus Gloop

Time treads water in the Blue Room, nearly drowns. Light comes up, blinds go down, we endure. A talk on dog breeding with Daniel and his bitches, Debbie gets crafty with crochet, and cinematography of the early twentieth century by somebody from Gower.

"And what did you think of that?" Nurse Tinkerbell always asks, after ushering the visitors out; but most of us have lost consciousness by then and don't know where to find it again. Peter Pan stays away. I caught sight of him once in the corridor. He was fat as a buttery bollock. He looked like Augustus Gloop. I smiled, he turned, went back into his room. My heart descended a scale in A minor and when the G came it cut sharp. Surprisingly sharp. What is life, after all, but scales in contrary motion, one hand going up, the other going down?

Gwen

Drafts

First draft.

Mon Maître,
My heart stopped yesterday at two o'clock in Les Deux
Magots. If you do not keep your promise you will be
responsible for the death of this artist. If you are sincere
when you say that I can produce great work it is your
duty to the world to keep your promise. I have it on
good authority from the horloger on Boulevard St.
Germain that if a clock is stopped for more than
twenty-four hours it will never keep true time again.
It jolts, sticks, gets ahead or behind. It slowly begins to
rust. A pendule must be kept well-oiled and in use to
stay true.
   Your starling.

Second draft.

Dear Rodin,
You say I am wild, childish, barely civilised. Would you draw me just this side of the fence, the way Augustus draws Dorelia? Or would you draw me outside the parameters of respectability, looking in? You say I take your energy, your teeth, your nails. Well, I can give them back to you. I keep them in a little box by the side of my bed. You say the winter fills you with chills and gloom. Come and see the sun breaking through the clouds as I undress. Come and hold spring in your arms.

Third draft.

Rilke says you lie down on the floor and listen to the gramophone with that woman. If you do not keep your promise I shall make a scene. I shall follow you to Notre Dame and I shall make a scene. Before God I shall make a scene. Edgar has just jumped in from the moonlight, left muddy pawprints on this letter to show his displeasure at you too.
Gwen John.

Moth

God

Drew tries to make love to me. I refuse for the first time in seven years of marriage. The guilt makes me angry.

"Fuck off and leave me alone. I'm exhausted. I'm thirty-two and I feel like forty-two and we haven't got any decent contraception. If I got pregnant now I'd have to consider a termination. And I don't want you coming off on the sheets either. Nothing dries in this weather."

I get up, look at the night sky. The stars have vanished like God's run out of sparklers. What are we all but little animals in his great big black magician's hat, pretending to appear, pretending to disappear.

Elizabeth

Westerns

Dear Elizabeth,

Boy am I sore. I've taken up football in rec. I mostly play on the line doing the dirty work – blocking, rushing the passes, that sort of thing. The side to side movements have my ankles and knees sore as heck. You know I've got the heart of an eighteen-year-old, but my body tells me I'm forty. Think I'll ever learn? Ha ha. These young guys that think they're hot, the old man surprised them some. It's fun to try to prove them wrong.

My cellie Buckwheat got a stay of execution while they wait on a case in West Virginia. It sounds good at first, but they can take a stay and go on and execute you. A stay is not completely safe. But I'm happy for him. I fully expected him to go. He honestly said I can't see myself growing old here and living the rest of my life here. Maybe it'll be for the best. He has a dream where he has ninety candles on his cake and he wakes up just before he can blow them out. You'd love Buckwheat. He's a no-nonsense, very honest, speaks from the heart guy. We watch westerns together. He's the guy who gallops up to the corral in a cloud of dust. I'm the guy laid back on the grass with a hat over my face, maybe chewing on a stick of gum. Kind of lazy. Kind of indolent.

Cardinals are kicking butt. A seven-and-a-half game lead. They stay real consistent and that helps. Seems like they're coming together at the right time. Our pitching staff is getting healthy again as well. That, my friend, is where the games are won and lost. Cardinals are probably one of the better defensive teams going. Defending and pitching are the two main ingredients of a championship team.

I had some words with the prison chaplain the other day. He said Moses was a basket case too, and then he parted the Red Sea. Makes you wonder what he's got in mind for me. As a great catcher from the 1950s team of the New York Yankees, Yogi Berra, said, "It ain't over till it's over."

I'm sending two pictures to you and you can keep them. These are my wonderful kids whom I love so much. I got them from Mary, my ex-wife. My daughter is wearing some make-up and a little lipstick — my baby's growing up!

God, I wish Minnie would visit.

Gwen

Preparing the Canvas

I prime canvases endlessly, try not to wait for you. Warm rabbit glue in a copper pan, add a little chalk, stir the mixture gently with a wooden spoon. Sometimes I let the liquid boil so that it fills with air bubbles that will leave little sinkholes in the linen. Apply to the canvas with a wide brush or cloth. Wipe clean. Repeat. Behold – a perfect canvas, an undulating skin ready to be coloured in.

Ida's Death

Augustus writes that Ida has died giving birth to their fifth
son. I send violets. She has gone to a cave where the air is
light and she can breathe, he says. Another cave, nonetheless.
What has she done since Slade? Have babies, cure freckles,
share my brother's bed with Dorelia. What has she drawn?
Absolutely nothing. Her head was too full of babies' cries.
There was not enough space for her own voice. She toasted
love at the end in Vichy water. I suppose it's all she had. I
bite my hands. We go to heaven in single file, one by one,
not with our lovers, our babies. They do not erect
monuments to people who have lovers and babies. They
erect monuments to people who paint something.
Something good. Poor sweet Ida.

Elizabeth

Colonising Mars

Time hovers in the Blue Room like a dragonfly over the meniscus. We are the algae, the meniscus, everything teeming beneath, within, seemingly stagnant on top. Sometimes it darts at us, merciful, quick, carries one of us off in its hinged mandibles.

"And shall we colonise Mars?" the visitor asks, an expert on orchids and climate change. "With packets of seeds?"

"Oh yes," the stephanotis claps. "Eleanor would do it. Eleanor would have done it. She carried seeds in an old clutch bag she bought in a Honiton antiques shop. She was a great one for the dahlias."

Everyone suddenly has a favourite flower to be saved from extinction.

"You can't beat roses."

"Bluebells."

"Snowdrops."

"I want troubadours in my wreath when I die."

"Marguerites."

"From the garage every time. And they were always fucking wilted by the time I got them in the vase."

"Oh my goodness, she said, don't you just love butter?"

"Dandelion's a weed."

My mind's a blanket. Flowers galorey my husband would bring the morning after, yet I can't think of a single one.

"Tulips."

Peter Pan wheels in, his face glistening with too much soap and too many sardines. "Hyacinths for me," he says. "Every time."

My heart ascends a scale in C major, no sharps, no flats. Keep your fingers curved as if you're holding a mouse. Don't let him go, don't let him slip.

Gwen

Notebook Entry

RULES TO KEEP THE WORLD AWAY.
Do not indulge in sensual reverie.
Do not look in shop windows.
Do not crave affection where none is to be found.
Work for one moment, work for eternity.

Letter From Rodin

My dear Gwen Marie,
My deepest condolences at your tristesse. I shall come to
see you tomorrow in the evening. Remember that life
and death revolve in each other's arms like dancing
partners.
   Auguste

Moth

Pot Noodles

I place Jamie's medication carefully in the fridge and turn up my Benefit High Beam cheek-illuminating smile. I can't wait for these boys to blossom under my parenting skills. A kind word, a bit of sympathy and compassion, that's all they need.

"So. It's a lovely day. Let's all get out for a walk in the sunshine with Mr Stinks."

"Who's that?" Max, a miniature Harry Potter complete with identikit lightning scar on his forehead, looks round warily like he expects some old tramp to come waltzing Matilda through the door.

"Our dog."

"Does he shit off all the time?" Jamie grins. "Does he fart in your face? I'll train him if you like. I've trained Max to pee into his own mouth. And he sucks my willy in the bath."

My two are giggling hysterically now, but I keep my Benefit High Beam smile on full power. These are shock tactics of course. I'm not in the least fazed by them. "Let's get going then."

"I'm hungry," wails Max. "I want my dinner first."

Jesus H, it's ten in the morning. "Did you have any breakfast?"

"Nah." Both boys bring a Pot Noodle out of their rucksack. "Dad always gives us these."

"Well, your mother's back tomorrow so things'll go back to normal soon I'm sure."

"She always gives us these as well, but not Bombay Bad Boy cos it's too spicy."

I boil the kettle, fix the Pot Noodles. Roan and Dove sniff the air longingly, but I remind them that they will be having a proper lunch later – fluffy cheese on toast à la Annabel Karmel.

Max's glasses steam up as he scoffs his chicken and mushroom at a temperature saints must burn at. The only other person I've known to do this is a girl in primary school who had green snot dangling permanently from either nostril.

"Yuk." I can't help myself as both boys tip their pots up to their lips to drain the last dregs of sauce. Jamie bends one eye on me while the other travels so far left I feel like I'm in the presence of Mad Eye Moody. Which is a bit of a worry; at the end of Harry Potter everyone cops it. It's a fucking bloodbath. Even poor old Hedwig blows up in a side car.

Elizabeth

Skinny Minnie/Eton Mess

I'm sitting on the wicker chair by the window when Minnie comes in. Looking at Caldey Island and the sea. I know she's there even before she speaks. She'd knock the air molecules out of the room, that one, with her presence.

"Nana."

"Minnie." I spin, tilt on my own axis. The world topples. "Your hair's pink!"

"Strawberry champagne, actually. With a hint of Bucks Fizz."

I laugh, stand up with my back to the window. It's the best way to look at a rainbow, with your back to the sun. She's wearing a dress like the petals of a sunflower and vintage winkle-pickers on her tiny, high-arched feet.

"You look … radiant."

"So you know then."

I nod. There's a slight curve of the belly, probably only discernible to me, to her mother. But she was always so skinny. Skinny Minnie, we called her. Skinny Minnie who could draw stallions and chaffinches at the age of three;

Skinny Minnie who was modelling at fourteen; Skinny Minnie with her Rapunzel gold hair and her beautiful bones.

She flops down on the bed and starts pulling at a loose patchwork thread. "I suppose you think I should get rid of it, too." Suddenly aggressive, defiant, as vulnerable as a child, though she has a fish in her tummy and a silver star in her nose.

"Of course not." I lean over and kiss the strawberry champagne. It smells like a kitten. "When are you due?"

"Christmas. I thought of Holly. D'you like it?"

"Yes, very much." I smile. We always know what sex we're creating. Either that, or we wish them into being.

"Mum says I'll never finish my degree, if I have her."

I tread around the landmines, wishing I had a protective helmet. "How is your mother?"

"Oh, you know."

Yes, I know. Fiercer than tigers, intricate as clocks. Always on the lookout for a new sunrise, a new ship.

"She's up for some award again."

A small bubble of pride, like a snow globe I shake occasionally. Watch the snow fall like dandruff onto my daughter's white coat, my son's strong yet scholarly shoulders.

"Anyway, I've got a job."

"Oh?"

"In a tattoo parlour."

It takes all of the strength in my wizened old body not to move a muscle. Strange how sometimes it takes more strength to say nothing, do nothing. At the still point, there the dance is, Peter Pan says. Like a tornado's heart.

"I've only done designs so far, and Chris says they're amazing. I can't wait to turn them into skin. When you think about it, it's the ultimate canvas. It's alive. It scars, bleeds, ages, shrinks, and the artwork just has to go with it. How cool is that?"

I invite her to stay for tea and cake. Peter Pan wheels in with a book on horticulture and a stench of rotting compost. She is very kind to him. Minnie is always kind.

So glad to know Nana has a friend in the home. So sad to make it short and sweet. Nick revving up the engine as we speak. Hours scouring Port Eynon for a little something for his parents. Lunch in Bath. Very posh. The seagulls, yes, bombarding us like kamikaze pilots. In the end a doorstop from a little old junk shop in the shape of a carousel horse. Dented in parts but vintage kitsch if you know what I mean.

I listen to her chittering on. Her colours refract, shimmer through the raindrops in my eyes. She's about to disappear. How beautiful, rare and brief rainbows are. They must be the prick teasers of the meteorological world, and the clouds like pot-bellied weak-bladdered old men scuttling after them.

"Bye, Nana. Love you."

"Love you too, Cheeks. It was wonderful to see you. Don't forget your folic acid, all the essential oils."

She winks, pokes her tongue out, winkle-pickers off, and the floorboards squeak in protest beneath her tiny, high-arched feet. *Don't go. Not yet.* How evanescent and selfish youth is.

"In the female dragonfly," Peter Pan pronounces from his wheelchair, "the maiden flight is always vertical. Then subject to the prevailing wind."

The wind. A slovenly old bag who farts beneath her party frock, whips a wig off her own head to reveal a bald moon staring down on a grim and grimy sea. Old cuttlefish, cola bottles, seagull smears. The rain pisses down from the pot-bellied weak-bladdered old men, and I wonder if the monks on Caldey Island ever eat their own ice cream. If, during a vow of silence, any of them ever scream. Or do they kneel for eternity in a row of tornado hearts, like artichoke plants.

Gwen

Sex and Sinkholes

He fades me like the sun. If I gaze too long upon him. I wriggle from beneath the thickened waist, step carefully over Edgar, who immediately jumps into my warm soiled space. Just like Dorelia. Warm the brown teapot, wipe the William Morris cup he admires, prepare some chestnuts in milk for his digestion. It scares me, sometimes, to think how old he is. He props himself up on a loose-tissued arm, watches me work.

"You are form in air, like a statue. You have no bad sides or angles. You are magnificent."

"Thank you." I pull on my white tunic nonetheless.

"You have made preparations." He indicates the canvases, the pictures of Fenella. "You have revealed the art of undressing. It is sad and sensual *naturellement* as all love is. It is an outburst."

I bring the chestnut milk, sit at the foot of the bed. "Directed at you," I challenge him.

He laughs, and I am suddenly angry that he is old, that Ida is dead, that my canvases remain unadorned, that I am so timorous of the world yet so desirous of its pleasures. "I'm the crumpled glove my master warms his thumb in when he chooses."

The lines on his forehead turn into calligraphy. "I came here to console you, comfort you in your grief."

"How very noble." I pull up my tunic, straddle the thickened waist. Edgar jumps down obligingly. Just like Ida.

My body buckles, undulates, overheats, fills with sinkholes, air bubbles.

"Your face is wetter than your minge," he chides.

"Does it bother you?"

"Not at all."

First he colours me, then he mottles, finally he bleaches.

Opening the curtains wide, I suck him in, absorb him, inhale him, exhale him. Inhale him, exhale him.

Even when he's gone and my eyes are closed, he goes on burning my retinas.

Elizabeth

Letter To Death Row

Dear James,
I'm Odette tonight. All feathers and glitter, and the
shapes I make you wouldn't believe. I spin, conduct the
air, twist and plait the atmosphere. From a distance
this life looks perfect like a set of veneered teeth, but
don't forget that underneath we've been pared down to
fit. Pared down to the bone, the stump. We're merely
groundhoppers really. Close to, we cry, pant, thump.
You'd be surprised how loud it is if you're sitting in the
pit. Our panda eyes as the greasepaint melts. Our
stepladdered tights and ladybird pumps as our sinews
strain, the toenails curl. Behind the ethereal being is a
surprisingly muscular heart.

Gwen

The Little Interior

"How can you love him?" L'Homme Femme demands, applying the calendula I brought for her scalded arm in fierce sharp dabs. "He's pompous shit. *Merde*. He's like a cathedral in awe of his own grandeur. Thinking his spire reaches up to heaven."

"Well," I giggle. "That's true. But in a hundred years' time his work will be in every museum in the world, still covered in thumbprints. Philosophers will have a *carte postale* of *The Thinker* on their desks. Lovers will have one of *The Kiss* on their dressing tables."

"And what about *your* work?" She pours cardamom tea from a pot the colour of faded pansies, decaying flowers. "What will become of that?"

I shrug, gaze about the room. The little interior so like my own: the round table, the teapot which from where I sit looks as if it has no spout, no phallic adornment, the paints, overalls, smock. How hard it is to create light and space for ourselves as women. I should like to paint so that the viewer has to work hard also to create light and space within my pictures. "My friend Ursula is an artist who lives with her parents. Sometimes she has to go into the middle of a field to scream."

"*Bien sûr.* We must be ruthless. There is no place for family. Or love."

I think of my father playing the organ every Sunday in Gumfreston, his foot firmly pressed on the tenuto pedal of grief. "If I could make a living out of my painting that would be a start. The rest I leave to others. But I think if I am left alone without distraction I can produce something good."

"So. Let the pompous turd shake at his own wonder. Start to tremble a little at yours."

Moth

Cunts and Flying Saucers

We trudge down the hill, Ro racing ahead with Mr Stinks. What a delight – a boy and his dog running through the countryside. Jamie whacks nettles with a big stick.

"If we had some string," his voice gleams, "we could have a conker fight."

"Absolutely not. No, no, no. We don't have any in the house."

"Everyone has string. You must be mental."

"Yes, we do have string." Dove pulls me up. "In the drawer by the sink in the kitchen."

"Oh, yes, sweetheart, we did. But Daddy took it to work this morning. Oh look, here's Cherry with her nana."

Nana Rottweiler is hurtling towards us with a pram so shrouded in shawls and blankets it's impossible to discern its contents. Jamie and Max charge up. Even Roan and Dove peer in tentatively.

"Fucking hell." Max steps back. "Have you been feeding her Bombay Bad Boy?"

"She looks very…" I fumble for a word like a stone in my pocket.

"Red?" Jamie offers, his magical eye travelling so fast I catch it with a grin.

"Well. She looks very well."

"Teethin', innit. Little cunt. Kept me up half the night."

"Oh dear. Well, we better get on. Lovely day for a walk."

"For them what's got the legs."

She puffs off and Ro falls in beside me, his face solemn.

"What does cunt mean exactly? I thought it was a swear word."

"Mo's just saying she's a bit cheeky, a bit naughty."

"Like Dove."

"No, not like Dove. Not at all."

Jamie hits Mr Stinks with his stick. "Cunt's a fanny, knobhead."

"Frou-frou," I correct. "Don't do that. It could hurt him."

"He likes it, see. He wants me to do it again."

"No, he doesn't."

"So there are lots of words for the same thing." Ro's interest is piqued. "Why is that?"

"I don't know. I suppose it's how the language evolves." I keep stumbling over the precipice of my own making. "Fanny in America, for example, means bottom."

"Fanny, fuck, cunt, cunt." Jamie gyrates his hips like he's having sex with an invisible nymph. I wonder suddenly if he's witnessed his parents at it or accessed some porno site.

101

Luckily I'm distracted from these horrific mental images by Dove grabbing my arm and pointing.

"Look," she squeaks, her eyes wide as flying saucers steeped in vodka. "Look."

Elizabeth

Moonlight

"Crudities and dip, Elizabeth. If they don't do the trick, we'll try a laxative."

"Thank you." I have a surprisingly muscular sphincter.

"Peter's on his way."

"Oh, good."

Peter brings a record to play on the gramophone Minnie gave me for my sixtieth. Vintage kitsch. It's pink, wind up, and the stylus wobbles in a zigzag pattern over the grooves. Peter has to steady my hand. Beethoven's *Moonlight Sonata*. Sad, faltering, slow, but it makes a change from Satie. We chew splinters of courgette with jalapeno dip. Peter starts to sweat.

"Phew." He smiles. "This is tropical heat."

"Very good for Alzheimer's, so my daughter informs me."

"Well, then, I must persist."

I smile and listen to the man who conducts moonlight, makes the stars shimmy. Peter's face looks like it's about to catch fire.

"He was profoundly deaf by this time, of course," he gasps. "The only music he heard was in his head. After a performance of his ninth symphony he couldn't hear the applause and, fearing there was none, he wept. Someone had to turn him around to see it. When he died there was a massive peal of thunder according to his doctor. I like to think it was God, shouting him a welcome. Making sure he heard the ovation. 'Well done, Ludwig. In you come.'"

I giggle, nearly choke on a cauliflower floret. I haven't giggled in ten years and Peter knows it.

"Don't stand on ceremony, man. Get yourself in here."

My cheeks ache.

"Everyone shout 'Ludwig'. One two three. Oh dear, he thinks we're saying earwig. Ludwig, get in here you deaf bugger. I haven't got all year. Christ, when I created a musical genius why the hell did I make him hard of hearing?"

My cheek muscles have gone, as has my sphincter muscle. Thank god for plastic knickers. The smell mingles with the smell of Peter Pan's colostomy bag, producing a new fragrance perhaps – vintage kitsch Minnie might call it.

"I love you." His voice is unnaturally loud. Like Beethoven's probably. The man who made the stars shake. How shall I react? What word shall I choose to continue the narrative of our lives? In a selection box of words shall I keep the soft centres for last, leave the chewy ones unwrapped, go to the next layer?

"Yes," I said in the past tense, remembering the moment hours later.

Gwen

Note to Self

Stop thinking about carnal relations, or at least have carnal relations with someone other than R. Anyone other than R.

Letter to Augustus John

Dear Augustus,

I escorted father round Notre Dame, the Louvre and the Eiffel Tower. It was a good visit. Then he went back to Wales. He's still much concerned about the weather and he still plays the organ every Sunday at Gumfreston.

I hope you are feeling a little better about Ida. I notice in your lyric fantasies you often depict her holding a bunch of violets not unlike the ones I sent on her deathbed. Strange how you take my ideas and present them as your own.

How is Dorelia? Do you still get her up in that ridiculous Romany attire? And does she still fulfil your romantic ideal or has she taken Ida's place completely now – flatfooted, earthbound, domesticated, babies grunting about her like pigs? Is she finding out how hard it is (as Ida did) to be wild and free yet still be able to nurture properly?

(Note to self – don't send this draft.)

Elizabeth

Perfect Turd

We eke out the days, Peter, Wendy and me. The sunlight stretches like an ageing ballerina *en pointe*, fearing the imminence of the final curtain. On Tuesdays we take tea al fresco on the bench by the ornamental pond. It's a small privilege allowed patients who are not completely delusional or dangerous. Cucumber sandwiches and scones, sometimes a pot of tea and jam. Peter Pan refuses any food that is pink or orange. His wife and the stains on her clothes put him quite off colour. A subdued palette, however, he eats with relish.

"Strawberries," Tinkerbell announces, putting up the camp table in front of us and spreading a blue-checked tablecloth over it.

Peter makes a face.

"Maybe a glass of white wine."

Then beams.

"As it's my birthday."

Exclamations at this. How old can Nurse Tinkerbell be?

"Twenty-one is it? Twenty-one again?" Peter's attempt at chivalry goes a little astray.

107

"Will it interfere with my medication?"

"Doctor's orders."

"Oh, how lovely."

The poor old crotchets and quavers stuck in the Blue Room with Satie floating around their heads.

"This is nice. A few boats on the pond and it's Henley Regatta."

"Oh yes, Eleanor went every year with a French hamper and a bottle of bubbly."

"Was it as wonderful as they say it is?"

"I don't know. I never went. I stayed back, looked after Bruno. Eleanor's cousin Rosemary once said, 'Dear Wendy, always so obliging.'"

"Destroying angel." Peter Pan consults his book on *Common Toadstools of the Great British Isles*. He points to the rotting fence surrounding the ornamental pond. "Jelly ears, elfin saddles, hairy curtain crusts if I'm not mistaken." He wheels away, waving. "I'm off in search of the rare *Pongchámbinnibóphilos kakokreasóphoros*."

Wendy's on her tenth sip. I've been counting. "Sometimes I think I've spent my whole life obliging. Smiling and obliging."

I catch up in sips. "I'm lucky if my son writes to me once a month. Some postcard from Nigeria where he's sorting out the Igbo tongue, whatever that is, after the mess the

108

missionaries made. Never a 'What's the weather like in Tenby, Mum?'"

"I hate to say it, but I don't think Eleanor always got it right. Jerry and I planned to be wed."

Light glimmers on the veins in a leaf.

"Until she put her nose into that. We used to … play ping-pong … up on the roof terrace behind the hydrangeas. One time we were in the middle of … ping-pong … when there was a most dreadful smell. They were frying onions for the chow mein special. Jerry made a carefree, grandiloquent gesture up there on the roof terrace underneath the stars and said, 'I shall let my wok burn.' It is something, isn't it, that a man let his wok burn for me."

What a waste. All this life reduced to a pencil sketch of two old women on a bench. I surpass her in sips, drain my glass like a clown fish. "Definitely. Definitely something." We giggle like schoolgirls, don't hear the soft split of the rotting fence as it gives way to Peter's wheelchair. Nor the deep plop as his body hits the water, submerges with barely a ripple like a perfect turd. The kind of turd that doesn't need toilet paper. Clean submarine. Our reminiscing hearts can't beat fast enough to save him. A pencil sketch of two old women on a bench, life and death going on behind them.

Gwen

My Despair Over the Inexorable Nature of Time and How We Cannot Ever Go Back to That Moment When All Potential Was There, When It Wasn't Over

Why does it fret me so that we change and age? Why does it fret me so that we can't hold on to that one luminous moment?

Moth

Foxes

In the middle of the off-road cycle track sits a fox like a shy red dog. When the sun hits its coat it could even be a golden retriever puppy. Mr Stinks is wagging his tail and sniffing him all over like he's thinking, yippee, fox shit to roll in soon.

"There's another," breathes Dove, and sure enough a second fox limps out from behind a tree trunk to join the first.

"His brother," Jamie asserts. "Have you got any rope?"

"Absolutely not." I ignore the look on Dove's face. "We definitely don't have any rope."

"You must be mental. Everyone has rope."

"Ssh." I put a finger to my lips. "We don't want to scare them. They shouldn't be out. Foxes are nocturnal. Does anyone know what that means?"

"They're zombies?" offers Max.

"It means they sleep in the day and come out at night. Something's wrong. Look how dazed and thin they are. This is a bit of an emergency, guys. We need to get home as fast as we can and ring the RSPCA. We've got a mission here."

I'm surprised by the children's response. The words emergency and mission have galvanised them. They all turn on a ten pence and start moving. Even Jamie has a *True Grit* look about him. That's all he really needs – a goal, a purpose. Something to dig his teeth into. (Enough of the Pot Noodles and porn.)

We speed back up the hill, overtaking Mo and fizzy pop Cherryade. I explain about the foxes as we pass.

"Vermin," she calls after us. "If Gavin still had his gun, he'd shoot 'em."

Dove starts to cry and I scoop her up for the last few paces. "Nobody's going to shoot them," I tell her. "We're going to save them."

Elizabeth

A Ceaseless Rumba

Dear James,
I am Ondine tonight, the watery sprite. I arabesque
from the sunless depths, take my first tentative steps on
dry land. My body's chalk, the rocks are dust, grass is
sharp as bait. I acquire a shadow from the burning
light, receive air like rain, kiss my mortal lover on the
lips. Drained of all life, he gasps like a fish. I've spent
too long in the deep to frolic now in the shallows. Peter
lies dead at my feet.

Gwen

Letter to Rodin

Mon maître,
I have sold Fenella *my nude girl to the Contemporary*
Arts Society, and the American collector John Quinn
has bought Girl Reading at the Window, *so I do not*
want for money at the moment. I nearly died when the
letter came addressed to Miss John, 29 Rue Terre Neuve.
"A five hundred franc advance awaits you at Brentano's
bookshop for any picture you care to send." He looks for
something he calls acid in the work he picks. Evidence
of pain and struggle. Well, I have certainly had enough
pain and struggle to warrant getting a little acid. He's
something of an eccentric apparently. He rides his horse
in Central Park every morning, takes castor oil, wears
rubber heels. He said he would get rid of his Picassos
for a Gwen John. Augustus is both pleased and peeved
at the outcome. I think he rushes too much in his life
and his work. It is all action and dynamism but little
reflection or meditation, which is so important, n'est ce
pas?

I realised I want to paint consciousness. Just as in your Thinker *you make the act of thinking theatrical, I want to make consciousness palpable. To suggest connections between objects and personality: the closed book, the open book, the window, the cat, the teapot, the diary. You think I am too high-flown. Well, perhaps I am.*

I followed you to church last week. I sat in a back pew. You didn't notice me. I barely heard the sermon. Was it light came first or was it the word? Surely it must have been light. I was busy sketching hats, plaits and backs. Oh, the baffling secrecy of a back. I am half in love with the little orphan girls and their snowdrop bonnets. Do you know why they sit on their hands? Well, I'll tell you. It is because they know that the hands reveal all, betray everything. Perhaps that is why you never finished Whistler's Muse. *Because you knew my hands would betray everything. Like the long fingers to the mouth in your* Farewell. *The fluttering speech of the hands. Do you really imagine you can spend the rest of your life without visiting me again? Without warming your thumb in my mouth once more? Without tasting the origin of all creation as you call it? If a woman undressing is like the sun coming out then your eye must be continually blasted by the naked*

115

models you employ to cavort and shove their pudendas at you. Your fucking whores. Strange how they change shape whilst working with you. Is that because you fuck them all? Is that because you fuck them into being pregnant? Is that how come you sculpted Eve cowering, hands over her belly? Cast out. Cast out of Eden. Your fucking whores.

(Note to self. Do not send this draft.)

Elizabeth

The Weight of Words

Peter's memorial. I wear black, Wendy plum. Someone is playing the bagpipes. It is monstrous, ludicrous. I feel quite sure Peter would have preferred Beethoven. He's to have a woodland burial. There's been much debate on the subject.

"Under a toadstool."

"Good for the agriculture."

"Lay where they fell in World War One."

"Should have left him in the pond where Martha tried to leave Harry, but he kept on screeching."

Peter's body arrives in what looks like a giant laundry basket followed by a solitary mourner – a man in jeans and tee shirt. Wendy starts giggling. "Dirty linen," she whispers to me. "I can't help thinking of dirty linen." There is talk of God and the resurrection, some dreary singing, praying, a creaking of knees. Somebody farts continually, possibly me. The man in jeans gets up to speak. He is very sunburnt like a fisherman.

"Peter Sillitoe, what can I say? A man of many words, as you probably know, and many talents. But what you probably don't know is that he as good as killed his wife."

Someone applauds like it's a piece of theatre. The rest of us lean forward, sick with excitement. This is soap opera come to life.

"Steady on," the vicar says, patting the man on the arm. "Remember where you are."

"He said he did his best. 'Oh, Herb, he used to say' – that's not my name, it's just what he called me – 'Oh, Herb, I did my best…'" (He is nodding now like a dog in a car window.) "But you didn't, Dad, you didn't. You could have stopped her and you didn't, and she was my mother."

We are creaking gates agape, ajar. Nurse Tinkerbell leads Herb off to calls of take care, mate, don't let it get you down. Man united in grief. The vicar takes up the eulogy but the words have lost their meaning with the wrong reader.

"Peter slept in a camper van after Nancy died on Kenfig Nature Reserve. Ate noodles, brewed tea. A common sight with his binoculars, conserving, collecting, collating. 'Oh, Herb' (my real name's Richard by the way) 'between the petrel and the porpoise, the wind cry, the wave cry.' He would quote T S Eliot. 'In the end is my beginning.'"

Afterwards there are sausage rolls and jam tarts. The piper eats five of each according to Wendy, and there is nothing under his quilt. I am garrulous with emotion.

"We were so busy gassing we didn't notice a thing. He tipped over, couldn't right himself with his weight. Gurgle,

gurgle, then it was curtains. Horseshoe – I mean Mr Smith the caretaker – fished him out and he was smiling. Not Mr Smith, I mean Peter. That's what made me really cross. Like he was happy to leave me, leave us behind."

Nurse Tinkerbell hands me a black notebook. "Herb, I mean Mr Sillitoe, didn't want it, so we thought you might like it, being an avid reader."

Peter's diary. I'm left holding the weight of words. The corpse of a man. Is that what we all boil down to in the end. A bunch of words. A few nouns, a connective, maybe an adjective or an action verb if we're lucky. Suck it. Suck it hard. That was an action verb, my goodness. And isn't it often the case that the important things lie in the addendum? Like Horseshoe licking the jam clean out of a tart leaving a crusty old dusty old shell, a small empty hollow where something good was. Where the heart lay.

Gwen

Young Nun

The young nun asks me why I want to become a Catholic. Her eyes are bright and remote as stars. I sit on a cane chair in a puddle of shadow, murky, tainted. I have prepared my answer.

"I want to subdue the extremes of my personality. Align myself with something good. With God. Generally my feelings are refined, sensitive, but sometimes I suffer from an excess of them. I'm overwhelmed by carnal desire."

She smiles, complacent in virginity, having given it all to God. What would happen if she died and found there was no God? What cry of desolation would escape those pale shrimp lips? Or would it matter? Is the striving all? Is the hoping all?

"I feel that the core of me is dark, that I am bad, unworthy, unable to love or be loved."

"He loves us all, even the sinners."

"But I want him to love me the most, love me the best. Don't you see?"

The young nun sighs – are we all in thrall to the same

master? – and her response sounds rehearsed. Is life just a series of empty gestures, grotesque poses?

"How can God compare a lion with a flower? He loves the different qualities in each of us."

"But what if there are no qualities to love?"

"You paint, don't you?"

"Yes."

"Well. Why not find God's love through the beauty of nature. Be God's little artist. God's little flourish."

"Oh yes, how nice. What a good idea." Empty gestures, grotesque poses. I sit in a puddle of hypocrisy, a bag of piss and shit.

"In fact, we're looking for someone to paint the founder of our convent, Mère Poussepin." She gets up, bustles about, her beautiful young body straining in the dove-grey uniform. I suspect that later tonight I will imagine myself a man, shoving God out of her mind and body with my dick. Please forgive me.

She hands me a prayer card of Mama Pussy. "If you're interested."

"I'd be honoured." I grin like a fucking ape.

Moth

Rope and the RSPCA

I shove Ro and Jamie in front of the Wii. They start playing a Harry Potter game, Jamie as Voldemort, of course, and Roan as Dumbledore (bad to his sister – hmmm…). Max kindly offers to help Dove colour her paper tablecloth with felt tips.

I Google the local RSPCA branch and punch in the numbers. Options: one for wings, two for scales, three for horns kind of thing. My ear is assaulted with canned muzak. Then a robotic voice informs me that the RSPCA relies heavily on public donations for its life-saving work.

Piss off.

That hedgehogs like cat food but it gives them diarrhoea.

Won't be giving them that then.

That every year the government is blackmailed by someone with a rabid animal.

Good.

That a brimstone butterfly looks like a green leaf.

Useful to know.

At last a real person answers. I explain about the foxes.

"They're starving, disorientated, possibly injured…"

"Not a lot we can do about that," the Right Shit Piece of Crap Arse replies. "It's not a situation we're equipped to deal with."

What sort of situation are you equipped to deal with – trick or treating? (I remember reading in the *National Enquirer* that if a paedo is found with a bowl of candy at Halloween he's carted off to jail. A stick or two of candy in the house is okay, but a bowl by the door and his number's up.)

"Foxes are becoming quite obnoxious," the Right Shit continues. "They rampage through the rubbish, squirt the garden."

Squirt?

"A woman reported a fox sunbathing in her conservatory bold as brass in broad daylight."

"Is there anything I can do?"

"Leave well alone. Survival of the fittest, I'm afraid. A badger'll probably get 'em tonight. Have you tried your local vets?"

I put the phone down. Jamie is shaking the remote like he's wanking and Max yells from the dining room like his scar's boiling with Voldemort's evility. Dove comes in with a comically shocked look. "He's coloured it all black. You're meant to colour the shapes, the mermaids and the unicorns. If you colour it all black you can't see the shapes."

The phone rings. I pick up, praying it's Drew checking in, but it's someone wanting to know if I know how much a funeral costs these days and would I like to put away for my own.

"No." I spin in my chair. "Right. All of you: out. Go and play in the garden. You too, Ro. Off you go. Out."

I Google the local vets, punch in the numbers. One for whiskers, two for claws, three for beaks type of thing. My ear is assaulted by canned muzak. Then a robotic voice informs me that I am in a queue but my call is important to them. At last a real person answers. I explain about the foxes.

"Have you tried the RSPCA?"

I breathe so heavily I probably scare the receptionist out of her straighteners.

"They're notoriously difficult to pin down."

"I gathered that. I was just wondering if I could bring the foxes to you."

"Oh no, it's illegal to transport a wild animal."

"Could a vet come and take a look at them?"

"Oh no, it's illegal for a vet to come out to a wild animal. A couple of years ago a vet came out to hunt for a lost duck, missed snipping a spaniel. He went on to impregnate ten bitches."

The vet?

"Can I give them some dog food?"

"Probably just give them diarrhoea."

"What can I do for them, then?"

"Best to leave well alone. Let nature take its course. You just can't help some animals."

I put the phone down. So I'm to leave the foxes to their fate, am I? Maybe Mo was right after all. Best off being shot, put out of their misery.

I get up, fix some lunch – fluffy cheese on toast à la Annabel Karmel. The smell brings the children drifting in. Jamie's first, a huge smile on his face. He's not a bad lad really. "D'you want your medicine now?" I ask gently.

"Not yet. You did have some rope." His voice positively shines. "In the shed."

Something tiptoes up my spine. Before I was married, a fortune-teller in Porthcawl told me I was a supersensitive. It's one step away from being a psychic. It means I pick up on things. "Roan," I shout, dropping a piece of Annabel Karmel. "Where's Dove?"

"Here I am, Mummy." She's by the outside tap, filling the dog's bowl. "I'm getting Mr Stinks a drink of water. He doesn't look very well."

I sprint up the garden. Mr Stinks is lying on the ground. Softly whimpering, barely moving.

Elizabeth

How's a Marriage Like a Hurricane?

Elizabeth.

Hi, dear friend. Glad to hear back. Sorry for your loss. It's hard to watch them slip away. I watched my grandad, and in the end the bills were astronomical. I think I had Cardinal baseball drilled in me by accident as I sat with him listening to games at a young age. The greatest Cardinal of all was I think Jack Buck, broadcaster and voice of the Cardinals. We struggled over the weekend. Lost two of three to Pittsburgh – damn the bad luck.

Our Sunday softball team needs one more win to capture first place. We easily have the best team because the other two captains haven't got a clue who to pick to win. They pick their cellie or their friend etc. I went after the fastest, the best gloves, bats, and more than anything the best attitude. I picked one guy I'm sorry for, but you can't be perfect. My idea on how to build a winning team is encourage each other, be positive, not with the ego kind of thing, and work together. There is no I in team. I look for the good in people rather than the worst. I'm a long way from perfect so how can I expect someone else to be? Let's have fun. If you're not having fun then there's no sense in playing.

Maybe it's time I do my job as a Christian and share a little with you. The Bible says I can do anything from Him who gives me strength. My cellie got me a sticker we put on the shaving mirror. God loves you but everyone else thinks you're a jerk. I've got another one too. How's a marriage like a hurricane? First there's lots of blowing and then you lose the house. I hope that sounds decent.

Your description of the ballet was really good. I can almost picture some of it. Nature has some super ways to show her beauty, but some like you can describe it. I walked the beach by the Gulf of Mexico one time. It was down on the west side of Florida, south of Tampa by Cape Corral or Fort Myers. It was peaceful. Something about the sound of waves really can bring peace to a weary mind. You have to listen for it, but it's there. I learnt to swim from a young age, and if I say so myself I was pretty decent. I also loved to dive off diving boards. I've had limited experience at much height, but I have dived between forty and forty-five feet. It was on a canoe trip, and man what a rush. Seemed like you could count the seconds before you hit the water. Other canoeists applauded me for my efforts.

127

Gwen

Me

Being what people expect.

By fear, following them.

Resolution.

No longer to shrink before people.

Do not let the world overcome you.

Try to ignore the unkindness of people, the impoliteness of people, want of money, ill health, my sins, pleasures of the world, fear of the world.

I Attempt to Justify the Choices I've Made

A beautiful life is one perhaps lived in the shadows, but regular, ordered, harmonious.

Moth

The Vet's

We sit in the waiting room next to an old woman with a ginger cat in a basket. Ro and Dove hold Mr Stinks between them. Roan is silent, his eyes like grass after rain. Dove half prattles, half sobs. "I'll never stop crying," she whispers in Mr Stinks' ear, "if you don't get better."

Jamie and Max are looking at gifts sold in aid of (how ironic) the RSPCA. Jamie farts a whoopee cushion incessantly and Max shines a torch at the ginger cat in the basket until the old woman asks me to tell my son to stop doing that please.

My son. Fuck off.

"Mr Stinks Dainty?" Thank God. But we really do need to change his name.

The vet is young with prematurely greying hair in a plait down his back.

"Why's he wearing a bobble?" Max whispers.

I babble the story about the foxes for the third time that day while the vet runs his nail-bitten fingers over Mr Stinks, murmuring, "Poor old lad, what have they done to you?

"Did the foxes attack him? He's got a nasty bite on his throat."

"I don't think so. They seemed so weak." Jamie is smiling, and I notice suddenly that his teeth are very pointed as if he sharpens them daily on something. "I'm not really sure. I suppose it's not impossible."

"He'll need a tetanus if he's not up to date. And a couple of stitches. There's some swelling too. Either his collar's too tight or someone's applied a ligature."

"What's a ligature?" asks Dove.

"A length of rope, possibly."

I do not even attempt to meet Jamie's wildly travelling left eye.

"I'll prescribe some anti-inflammatories and painkillers. He'll probably find it hard to eat for a few days. Poor old lad, what have they done to you? I'm afraid to say that this is the sort of case that almost needs reporting to the RSPCA."

You're fucking kidding me.

"But as he's in such good condition apart from that, I think we'll put it down to misadventure."

Half an hour later Roan carries Stitches (as we're calling him now) out to the car.

"Job done," smiles Jamie, his voice positively radiating light. "That's what my mum always says afterwards. Job done."

Afterwards? After what?

131

Elizabeth

Regrets/Shade/Old Apples

We sit by the picture window, Wendy and I. Light glides in furtively revealing the floorboards at our feet. Peter's diary on my lap full of the meals he cooked for his wife – the chocolate puddings, the drizzle cakes, banoffee pies, the roast dinners, the steak tartares. All with grades and whether they stained when she threw them up on her clothes. Lists and endless lists – like he got scared of using verbs so he just put down the nouns. The nouns surrounding the verbs. Agitating them.

Wendy bites into an imaginary apple, opening her mouth wide and clamping down. It's what ancient Hollywood stars do apparently to prevent jowls and sags. I try tentatively, opening my mouth wide then clamping. Horseshoe, who is mending the rotten fence by the ornamental pond, stares up at us for a moment. What can he see? Two gurning old women in a picture window. At least I have my own teeth and tits. Sometimes Wendy retracts her lips like she's Snow White being offered a poisoned one.

"Sometimes I wish I'd never met Eleanor." The light is

glaring at the wrinkles etched into her skin. Too bright. Too bright. Too bright for our weak old eyes. "Since Peter died, I've been thinking about her a lot. How in many ways she ruined my life."

"Apple bobbing." I try to distract, innocent as Eve before that fatal scrumping. "Did you ever do it? My late husband had an abiding memory of Halloween. He had a friend round, and his father, Bampa, the blithering idiot, ducked the boy's head in as a joke. One of his jokes gone too far, and the boy, irate, chased him round the room with an apple." I laugh at how we laughed at the memory.

"She bullied me, you see. 'Oh, Wendy, could you wash up while Rosemary and I entertain the guests? Oh, Wendy, could you walk Bruno? Oh, Wendy, the garden needs a little weeding…'"

"I think you loved her, and I think in her own way she loved you too."

Wendy smiles. The welcome relief of shade. Of grey. Of rain. "Just before she died she opened her eyes and said 'Dear Wendy'. That must mean something, mustn't it?"

"Definitely." My heart fills the gap between what I think and what I say. How many times did my heart do that? Inflate like a red balloon to fill that cavity, that empty space.

We bite in unison like two ancient Hollywood stars. But does biting count if you're doing it to an imaginary object?

Is it still an action verb? Fair play to Eve. At least she got a taste of the real thing. What is life after all but the biting of imaginary apples?

Gwen

Working

My delight upon hearing the cock crow as it signals the start of a day spent painting. Without interruption. Just a cup of tea and asparagus quiche and a day spent painting in my room, Edgar purring contentedly in his basket. Oh that my art may become my salvation, my redemption, the transformation of all my sins.

Girl in Profile

Spent all day on *Girl in Profile*, and I asked myself a hundred times did I want the mauve ribbon in her hair. And then in a tremor of agitation I scratched it out. Sometimes I feel I shall go mad. Sometimes I think this solitariness is mere obstinacy.

Moth

Monopoly

I'm sitting playing Monopoly with Dove getting all the pink ones like Pall Mall, when the phone rings. It's Adam. My heart right hooks my ribs. Is that how the first Adam felt when God made Eve? Hellboy is polishing the brass knocker quite calmly today, though yesterday he kicked the recycling bucket so hard down the street it broke.

"There's a photographic exhibition on at Cardiff Museum next week."

Dove moves the top hat to green. Takes a five pound. Sensible girl. Going up a level. Drew just buys up all the utilities. Well, he would, wouldn't he? Pushing the dog with his hammering spirit level hands.

"I thought Roan might be interested."

"Roan's at school." As you know.

"Oh."

"But I'd love to come. With Dove."

"Shall we say Monday?"

Hellboy's polishing the windows now. All the better to see how green the grass is on the other side.

"Yes." I put the phone down. Throw a six. Sail my ship up to Mayfair. Out into the blue. The wide blue infinity.

Elizabeth

Wendy Dies

Satie floats in from the Blue Room. Sad, faltering, abruptly stops. I can no longer hear the tick-tock of a melancholy heart. Wendy dies as the tourists leave this seaside resort – just as she wanted. Is it the word I feel when I feel this feeling goodbye? Goodbye, my friend. I hope the light is not too bright.

"We fully expected her to go," Nurse Tinkerbell said. "She did well to last so long. And to cheer us up, a talk on cats. If we're lucky, we'll have our own ginger tom."

Gwen

Met a Man

Last night I went to Les Deux Magots. Met a man. We took the train to Meudon. There wasn't much conversation. He led me into the back of a neglected garden. Pulling down my undergarments he knelt and licked. Then he penetrated me against the trunk of an old oak tree. Looking up at the sky I saw no stars.

Mon maître. Why hast thou forsaken me?

Met a Woman

Last night I went to Les Deux Magots. Met a woman. We took the train to Meudon. There wasn't much conversation. I led her into the back of the neglected garden. Pulling down her undergarments I knelt and licked. Then I penetrated her with my fingers against the back of the old oak tree. Looking up at the sky I saw the young nun's eyes.

Mon maître. Why hast thou forsaken me?

Met a Man and a Woman

Last night I went to Les Deux Magots. Met a man and a woman. We took the train to Meudon. There wasn't much conversation. I led them into the back of the neglected garden. Pulling down their undergarments I knelt and sucked and licked. Then they penetrated me against the back of the old oak tree. I couldn't look up.

Oh, *mon maître*. Why hast thou forsaken me?

Moth

Maggie

Steven's right. Maggie appears to have no neck. Her head's pressed against her right shoulder like she was some child genius on the violin. On the upside, I guess she can meet he who must not be named's left eye.

"Were they good?" she asks hopefully as the kids mill about waiting for the bell. Roan is talking to Jonah. He who must not be named is grappling with Cariad Jones, a freckled and rather corpulent girl from year six.

"Not bad," I lie, squeezing Dove's hand. "You're looking…" I fumble for the word like a stone in my pocket.

"Different," Dove offers.

"Well. You're looking well."

"The thing is," her voice lowers to a whisper, "sometimes I wish I was back in hospital."

"I can understand that." Voldemort has thrown Cariad's coat into a puddle.

"It was so quiet, so peaceful."

And is stamping on it.

The headmistress, Miss Grimbleby, comes out and yanks him by the ear. "Jamie's mum?" she calls out.

I pretend not to hear, and Maggie obviously can't with her head pressed against her neck, though I notice she makes a hurried bid for the gates, almost bumping into Rhys' grandad.

"Not long now for you." He waves his zebra stick at Dove.

"No, not long." I squeeze again, to encourage her of course.

We walk down the hill with Maggie.

"Steven wants to try and get back to the States," she tells us. "They have better facilities there for people like … Jamie."

What, like death row?

"I'll miss you. If you go."

We stand outside the chip shop where her black Mini is parked.

"The thing is," her voice lowers to a whisper, "sometimes I wish the tumour would come back. I know it sounds stupid, but it made me feel sort of special. People seemed to worry about me a bit."

I stare at the grey hair curling in that strange way hair does after chemotherapy, remembering the sleek black bob she used to sport. "It doesn't sound stupid. Are you sure you can drive?"

"Yep." She gets into her Mini. "I can see round the corners now."

We laugh and wave away.

"Why does Jamie's mum want to go back into hospital?" Dove asks.

"They have tasty food in hospital."

"Do they have fish fingers and green custard?"

"Probably."

I hold her hand very tight as we cross the road. Suddenly my eyes are stinging like mad.

Elizabeth

Death

Dear James,
It seems to me we teach children to count through
metaphors of death. The speckled frogs that fall off logs
after eating the most delicious grubs, the monkeys
falling out of bed, the ducklings that swim away and
don't come back. They don't come back. We go one by
one with our doubts, our fears, our regrets, our loose
ends, hoping death will tuck us in, hoping there are
beds.

Gwen

My Property

I bought that house in Meudon, with the neglected garden.

Elizabeth

What are Days For?

Days pass by, full of nothing. A glass of red wine. A soap opera. And what happened to all the characters? What happened to him? What happened to her? What happened to that one? In the end, all narratives twist into one. All women become one woman.

Gwen

The Strange Form

Turn gently back to your work. Take a leaf, a flower, study the strange form. Become God's little artist, God's little flourish. Be a saint in your work if you can't be in your personal life. Too much vanity. Too much care for material things. Too much sensual reverie. I have said my prayers. I have fed the cat. I have tucked myself in. I have re-achieved a state of innocence. I should like to go and live somewhere where I meet nobody I know until I am so strong that people and things could not affect me beyond reason. Leave everybody and let them leave you. Only then will you be without fear.

Technique

Observation:
The strangeness, colours, tones, personal form.

Execution:
Mixing of colours, lines in pencil, background, personal form out of background.

Moth

That Argument Carousel

I wash, Drew dries. Ro's in front of his Wii and Dove's colouring in a mermaid on her new paper tablecloth. I enjoy these quiet interludes, Drew and I bent over a household task. I tell him about the photographic exhibition in Cardiff.

"What sort of photographs? Snapshots of people's lives?" He takes a dishcloth, poses ridiculously.

The crack of grin I exhibit sets him off. We have hot guy at the oven in apron, hot guy cleaning his teeth, hot guy doing a dump pose…

"I don't know how you have the energy. I think the photos will be a bit more sophisticated than that. Adam thought Roan might like them."

"Adam? Roan's at school."

"I know. I said I'd come with Dove."

His eyes are cool as a cucumber left in the fridge too long. Frozen in the centre. A little wet at the edges.

"I wish I had time to go about to exhibitions."

And off we go on our old carousel of love and hate. He takes the chestnut Resentment and I hop on the dapple grey

Taken for Granted. We must look like idiots, sound like idiots, chasing each other round and round, never catching up, never gaining ground. Roan turns up the volume on the Wii, Dove's pen goes through the tablecloth.

Yes, I've been looking after children for the last ten years, any fucking idiot can do that, can't they? You don't need a brain, you don't need any physical stamina, never mind that I've produced two super brainy, super beautiful kids – that's just chance, sheer fluke, nothing to do with the spinach I ate, the walks I walked, the birthing balls I rolled over, the fanny exercises I did, and I got through it all without a blemish to my body, not even a varicose vein, a single stretch mark, and believe me that's no mean feat considering the other women I've seen with their tits down to their cunts and their stomachs like road kill.

I'm so fucking angry I could punch the lights out of the stars, and I chuck the milk bottles in the recycling bin by mistake, which reminds me I have to pay the milkman tomorrow. That's the kind of thing I have to hold in my head. If Drew had to do that his head would fucking explode. His dinner plate's so full, getting up and going to work in the morning. How fucking awful having to get up every day and trot off in your little white van stringing up the lights in some attic. I wish one day you'd get fucking electrocuted – whizz bang, off you go – then I could go to all the photographic exhibitions I want, and I could have sex with whoever I wanted without feeling any guilt, and the mortgage would be paid off, which would be an added bonus. Sorry, Drew. Sorry, God. I didn't really mean that. Maybe a small *zzzzz* just to jolt some respect into you.

And now I've stepped in dog shit taking out the recycling, so I suppose I'll have to clean that up, even though it's not my job, under the outside tap, which comes on and off like it's got a massive prostate, which reminds me I've got to pay the water rates. That's the kind of detail I have to hold in my head. If Drew had to remember that he'd probably discombobulate. He thinks he can see the big picture without studying the minutiae. Well, you can't. You have to study the minutiae very very hard if you want to see the big picture.

Elizabeth

The Truth

Dear James
I am very old. I live in a home. I was never a ballerina,
I was a mother. But do not think training to become a
mother is inconsequential. There is sweat, sweat and
more sweat. Behind every ethereal being is a
surprisingly muscular sphincter/frou-frou/heart. My son
makes documentaries. My daughter is a scientist. They
flew so high and sang so loud and I'm just a stale old
fart they shut the door on. Keep the door shut. Keep the
door shut. Reducing, reducing to a room, to a book, to
a picture, to a box. Don't let her out. Did you know
Margot Fonteyn never had any children? Anna Pavlova
never had any children. How could they fly with all
that weight?

Gwen

Regrets

Children's faces are secretive, mysterious. Their beauty is in the potential, the yearning. I sketch them in broad, thick, innocent strokes. Sometimes it makes me sad to think they will always be remote to me. They will never be mine.

My Garden

I cultivate my garden. Prepare the soil. Dig deep. Break up the hard, proud clods. Pull the sinewy, tightly bound weeds. Rake and sift till it's fine grained as flour. Plant the good seeds. Tend. Water. Nurture. Await the sun, the birdsong. I'll arrange flowers so you won't know where the vase starts and the blooms end. I'll achieve such a state of grace that you won't know where my body starts and my soul ends.

Moth

Not Deep Enough for Snow Angels

We get lost in the light blue gallery, the dark blue gallery, the dove-grey gallery. Squeaking and giggling over the parquet floor. A black-suited attendant puts her finger to her lips and tells us that if we leave our bag on the bench she won't be responsible, which defies logic even for me.

We stop by a painting of a Japanese doll with very big feet.

"Has she come out of the musical box?" Dove whispers.

"Probably. She can't dance until the music starts."

And a picture of the artist's room covered in a gauzy membrane of light like vernix.

"Hi."

It's Adam wearing a buttoned white shirt. Smart yet casual, same as me. Smelling very clean, just in case. Same as me.

"Gwen John. She had an affair with Rodin."

"Who?"

"The French sculptor, Rodin. Haven't you heard of him?"

"No."

"Did you get an education?"

He's an intellectual; the ghost of my mother chills the hairs on my neck.

"It was a very passionate affair, though a little one-sided. Look at this one, *Girl in Profile*."

I look at a picture of a girl with a turned-up nose and pink tones in her hair like Tonks from Harry Potter.

"She drew in a mauve ribbon then changed her mind and scratched it out. Didn't do a very good job though. You can still see it."

I peer hard, struggling to see the details. Yes the ribbon's still there. I imagine the process of painting, regretting, scribbling out.

"Why not just repaint in a glossy new colour?"

"We're not talking Dulux in those days," he smiles.

"Yes, but why leave evidence of the mistake?"

"Maybe she wanted to show her flaws. Maybe she thought her flaws could be beautiful."

He's licking me out and I can barely breathe. This is obscene.

"D'you want to get a coffee?"

"Oh, yes please."

We trot down the stairs, past a statue of Perseus with the head of Medusa – yuk – to the cafeteria, where Adam orders a latte (I feel very cosmopolitan) and an apple for Dove.

"Shall I chop it up?"

"No, I can just bite into it, Mummy."

We sit on a table next to two middle-aged women, one very hunched, talking about their dog, Bruno, and a man reading a bird-spotting book. I wonder if people think we're a family and the thought kind of pleases me.

"Whenever I come to Cardiff I'm always surprised how the pavements are buckling with tree roots."

"Roots too big for their boots," I grin.

"Oh, very good."

We stare at each other. Those hands. Those eyes. That hair. We're making love already in the dark-blue gallery. I'm unbuttoning that white shirt by the thumb-smudged statue of *The Earth and Moon*. In front of onlookers.

Dove nibbles at her apple.

"What do you do? Apart from looking after the kids."

Apart from guiding their spiritual, physical, mental growth? Apart from keeping everything in my head from their haircuts to their shoe size, their IQ to their eyesight? Every atom of their cells' health. Whether they should do Mandarin or Cantonese, ballet or t'ai chi. Whether I'm too controlling, not controlling enough. Whether in the end I'll fuck them up. "Nothing."

"But you must have done something before. Wanted to do something."

"I wanted to be a dancer."

"Oh, of course, you've got the body for it."

He has to say that. He has a little bit of cream above his top lip like in those romantic films, and the person has to indicate that there's a bit of cream on the top of the other person's lip but they can't find where it is, so in the end the person has to wipe it for them in that intimate caressing way. But he just wipes it with the back of his hand and the moment's gone.

"My life revolves around the kids."

"So where do you fit in?"

I'm the crux, the fulcrum. The piece of the jigsaw without which you can't see the picture. I'm the small detail without which their lives make no sense. "I don't know."

"Don't you want to find out?"

"I guess so."

"Look." His hands touch mine. Those long-fingered hands. The woolly mammoth must feel that touch in the frozen pipes of the ice age.

Dove bites her apple and spits the pips, and I feel the drunkenness of all things.

"I'm going to Tenby next weekend. I was wondering if you could get away."

Get away? I haven't got away in nine years. How can I get away now? What excuse could I give? Who would brush their teeth properly? Their hair properly? I think of Drew on the mat ready to comfort them if they wake from a nightmare and I know I can't take this step. My whole body is suffused with Drew and these children. How could I forget my history with them even for an instant?

"It's like that ribbon," I say in the end, after those smashed sapphire eyes have penetrated me again and again and again in a Tenby motel overlooking the sea. "You can scratch it out but it's still there."

We're done before we've begun and he knows it. "What about the photographs?"

"You see them. I don't need to." I don't need to see pictures reminding me of my own life, reminding me of lives I'll never have.

I take Dove's hand and walk out of the museum. Snow is falling, frosting Lloyd George punching the air and two children trying to make snow angels, but it's not deep enough for that yet. Not deep enough for snow angels. It falls like the sound of a small animal scurrying home. In my white shirt I'm camouflaged. Invisible.

Elizabeth

Cigarettes are Cool

Hi young one,
Hope things are in your favour. We had a little
excitement here as nine guys got locked up over a kite
(letter) someone put in to staff. Supposedly a plan was
being made to assault the chaplain, our unit manager,
and one officer I believe as well. Three people anyhow.
Conspiracy to commit a felony is what they're in
suspicion of. Most of the nine people were Muslim and
they thought the chaplain had it in for them. The
chaplain can be a jerk who thinks we shouldn't be
allowed anything. I don't care for him, but I sure don't
want him hurt or dead. To be honest, he came down
on all the religions here. He has no favourites.

The Christmas season is upon us. It gets crazy as heck
over here with all the shoppers, people decorating inside
and out with lights, lamps, sleighs and reindeer. There's
a lot of time and money spent on decorations and such.

Sounds like my dad's not doing real well. My aunt
keeps me up to date on him. He refuses to have anything

to do with me as well as my kids. Spent his life smoking cool cigarettes, when he got about sixty he wound up in hospital with gallstones. Doctor told him then if you want to live a little longer he needed to quit. It's your choice, live or die, it's up to you. I should add he drove a truck, and it was as much a nervous habit as well as a physical. I'd say he smoked between 4 to 5 packs a day. I don't remember him without a cigarette in his hand or mouth. Never had much to do with my brother or me. He's got emphysema bad, and he's on oxygen. He's a likeable guy, but he never took care of the ones who'd take care of him one day. I hate to see him suffer, but we all make our choices then we have to live with them. How well I know that.

Around here you get a little stir-crazy. I read and write, listen to music on my iPod. My ex-wife writes me once in a while, she never speaks of my kids or my relationship. She tells me how they're doing, sends me a few pictures. She said I could call but I had to pay for it. I guess it's a sad world all round. Guess I'm done rambling…

Gwen

Gloria

The girl in a blue dress brings eggs and milk from the farm. I call her Gloria though it is not her real name. But she is glorious. She has the kind of beauty that could live in a sonnet – that dark wing of hair, the straight brows, heavy lidded eyes, lily delicacy of skin. She is so fresh she reminds me of a clean-swept room. Promise of a new day. The chortling dawn. Her lover is a soldier. But he will not return, she says, which is why she wears blue – his favourite colour. Wherever he is, we are looking at the same sky. She has cried a river of tears over him. I shall paint her waiting for her lover, her soul and body dry as chalk, her dress the riverbed.

Moth

Punching Air

"Did you get an education?" The words still bite me and I spend the rest of the week researching Rodin and Gwen John. Order thirty-two postcards of the *Kiss* and then, two days later, thirty-two postcards of *Girl in Profile*. Show them to Drew.

"Why thirty-two?" His eyebrows are halfway over his scalp.

I shrug. "My age."

"So you're telling me," he sighs, "that by the time you're sixty-five we'll have a hundred and thirty of these fuckers in the house?"

I try to laugh but I can't and, seeing the look on my face, Drew does the clichéd thing and takes me in his arms.

Gwen

Spinsterhood

To persist through all wrong turnings, dead ends, false starts, set backs. TO PERSIST IS EVERYTHING.

I'm so fucking lonely. I WAIT AND WAIT FOR GOD'S GRACE AND HE DOESN'T SHOW UP. HE DOESN'T COME. HE DOESN'T WRITE ANYMORE. HE IS TOO OLD AND DECREPIT TO GET IT UP.

I'm a middle-aged spinster. Uptight. Loose down there. Very loose. Oh God, give me some moral fibre.

Moth

First Day

Gruffalo rucksack. Plaits. Slightly too large uniform. New shoes. I flick an imaginary speck from her red cardigan.

"I wish I was coming with you."

"You can't. You're an adult. You're not allowed."

"I know."

"You will be a little bit bored. You will walk Freckles," (we settled on Freckles), "probably have a cheese sandwich for lunch. I will have fish fingers and green custard."

"Probably."

We stand aloof amidst a maelstrom of mothers shouting, weeping, wailing, snotting – not to mention the children. When it's time to go, Dove allows me to pat her on the head then walks quickly to the open door. I raise my hand to wave, but she doesn't look back. I strain to see beyond the door. I think that's her hanging her coat and bag on the peg. Her small shape moving away down the long dark corridor. To a new world. As if all her life's been leading to this point. This new world. This death.

Turning to go, I remember how she kicked like fuck in

the stomach. Testing her boundaries, her parameters. Wanting to get out even then.

Elizabeth

Meds

The urge I got every spring to go mushroom hunting. You may not have them over there, but in warm wet weather it makes the mushrooms explode out the ground, and for a few weeks every spring there's a mad rush in Missouri to go and pick mushrooms. They're the best eating thing on the planet. At least a lot of Midwest USA people think so. I used to turkey hunt every spring and fall as well, and fish some in the summer. I was active once a year round fourth of July in our annual illegal hand fishing get together. Like I say, changing seasons I'm reminded of my past life.

13 inch TV, a radio, and two tubs stuffed full. That's all I got now.

Even though the Bible says how beautiful heaven is, it's tough to give up this life we have on earth. One day I'm ready, next day I have my doubts.

Mary my ex-wife is struggling to get by. Two teenagers are expensive. Another year, John starts to drive and Skyla in two. Car insurance is high and I don't want the kids suffering any more than they have. My way of helping would be to go on the way I'm headed. That way they could draw social security benefits. They can't draw if I'm alive. Besides, my case was so grotesque or brutal that there isn't a jury around that would forget seeing that. Give me involuntary manslaughter or murder second. Plus for armed criminal action I've got two twenty-year sentences that have to be served as well. Diminished capacity could bring a charge as low as involuntary manslaughter or as high as murder second, which is paroleable as well, but I'm sure it wouldn't come back as murder one – but even with a murder second it would be a lot of years. Going my way would at least get the kids raised.

The kind of peace I feel doesn't come from medication. We get as impatient as heck and God just laughs at us because he knows.

They locked my cellie up because his antenna was broken. He broke it that morning cleaning house and they locked us all down and he never had a chance to report it. He's looking at rule 3, dangerous contraband, which means nine months to a year in the hole. He and I had grown real close. He brightened my day and was upbeat and positive. That's another reason I don't want to spend the rest of my life here in prison. Life here is so unstable. Buckwheat would never hurt no one. Someone would use the antenna as a knife or a shank to stab someone, but Buckwheat never would as he's a super person.

There's a lot I never got to do like cliff diving in Acapulco or swimming and snorkelling or scuba diving in the Caribbean or the Bahamas. I never noticed how much water had to do with my life. I guess being raised by the mighty Mississippi had a long-term effect on my life. I was always at home in the water, swimming like a fish, only I had to surface to breathe once in a while.

Ex-wife and kids are coming to see me Friday. It'll be behind glass, I won't be able to hug them or shake their hand, but I'll get to see them nonetheless after three years. I kind of feel like I need to tell them something that will stick with them the rest of their life. I guess 'I love you' will probably have to do. I'm sure by now they know I screwed up...

It was super, but after they left and I got back into the housing unit, it occurred to me that they still carried the same expressions on their faces that they had when they were little. John would make Skyla a little mad and she'd have that same mad look on her face she had when she was little. How glad I am that I was a part of their life at least for a while. It was truly a blessing.

Things have moved on with my case finally, and they have now locked me up. At 2.30 p.m. to be exact. They've set the date for 12.01 a.m. Wednesday week. It shocked me a little, but I've known it was coming. I don't think you're ever ready for something like this even when you know it's coming. I'll take it as it comes though. Mizpah.

Cardinals trying to catch the Arizona Diamond bucks for home field advantage.

Have you ever ate pumpkin blossoms? My aunt fixes them real good. In your country, do you all raise soybeans and field corn? Over here in Missouri, Illinois, Iowa, Indiana and Nebraska, we have miles and miles of them both. The Midwest is also referred to as the corn belt, which is where most of our corn and beans are raised. I was thinking about pumpkin blossoms and it got me thinking about your country.

I really couldn't afford the meds on the street, but then again I really couldn't afford not to buy them either.

Not a lot going on here except time.

So jazzed up with medication I couldn't tell you where I was, but Ma said we spent a few years in the UK. Dad ran off and set up a new family. The first one didn't measure up in his eyes.

Gwen

Flowers and Cats

Rodin,

I suspect that this shall be the last letter I shall write to you.
You're not going to receive a letter from me ever again. If
you do not want to visit me then that is your choice, but I
should like to say that I think it is the wrong choice. If I
did anything to offend you in the past then I am sorry. I
didn't mean it. At least, if I meant it then, I don't mean it
now. We are both a little more âgé than we were. I, as you
predicted, am a spinster who arranges flowers and keeps
cats. You are the great man who will be buried with the
statue of the Thinker in your pocket. Blasting your way
into immortality. Imagine if I'd gone back to Wales. Spent
my days in a Welsh valley, the mountains closing like seas
over my head, my life cupped like a canary's in blackened
hands. I would never have met you. Never have felt you
mould my soul with your short, strong, slippery fingers.
Without you, I would have just been singing in the dark.

(Oh Gwen, Gwen, do not send…)

Elizabeth

The Truth

Dear Elizabeth,

Thank you for the truth. The truth shall set you free, Jesus says. It sounds like you've done a lot of good in your life. It's my turn now I guess. I stabbed my girlfriend twenty-six times. Before she died she managed to write my name in blood on the floor so they could track me down. Afterwards I just drove around till they got me. The prosecuting judge made a big thing of me taking my shoes off and creeping into the house, saying it was premeditated. I suppose it was. I knew she was going to leave me and I wanted to stop her. I guess I went about it the wrong way. It'll take me seven minutes to die in the chamber of execution. They'll give me an injection first to put me to sleep then some potassium chloride to stop the heart. There will be onlookers pressing their faces to the glass. My girlfriend's family will applaud when I go. I don't blame them. God bless you…

Gwen

Fuck Off

Dear Rodin,
This is the last letter I shall send. Oh, go to fucking hell.
Go to hell with your bag of clay and God's piss and
sculpt a few fallen angels for yourself. Fuck those singed
and hairy cunts while you're burning up. Off you go
now.

Moth

Just Because I Can

Amazing how much grime accumulates in nine years of children. I'm a whirlwind of dishcloths, soapsuds, rubber gloves, elbow grease. I do more in two hours than I've done in two years. And I get a lunchbreak. Cheese sandwich, cup of tea, banana and biscuit. Wonder if she's having fish fingers. Take Freckles for a walk in the land of sniffs and smells. Feel the rain on my face without having to discuss it. My hands deep deep in my pockets. It's so very quiet.

The house is so big. I do a dance move in the kitchen just because I can. Spread out on the settee just because I can. Soak my feet in an old herbal teabag, trim and shape my fingernails because hands and feet are the first to go. Beware ye women BC. Hands and feet are the first to go.

Rearrange the coffee table. It's so elegant. Wave at Hellboy rubbing his brass knocker. Nana rushing back home because little cunt's done a shart. I'm a glossy advert for the perfect wife and mother in my shiny as a new pincushion house.

I drive to collect Dove, planning my jobs for tomorrow.

Elizabeth

Maximilian

The last few moments of his life are captured on film footage. It's all on the CCTV of the Golden Gate Bridge. His body was so broken up underneath that we had to check it to make sure it was him. There he was, strolling along … small, dark-haired figure … puts something in his mouth – a stick of gum I think, though why you take a stick of gum to stop smoking when you're going to kill yourself…? He just looks like a guy strolling leisurely up and down. Then suddenly, real quick, he sits up on the side and back rolls off. It's real graceful, real beautiful, like he's taking a back flip off a high board. What got me was how he was just leisurely strolling then, as if he got the guts, up and made a dash for it before he could change his mind. I don't know why he did it. He never got over my dad leaving I think. God bless us all.

Thank you for giving me some of your time. Thank you for not turning your head away. Thank you for bearing to look beneath the surface.

Gwen

Pale Quiet Songs

I have told John Quinn that I would like my paintings to be hung next to each other. They do not need frames and just short, self-explanatory titles (like *Girl in Profile*) are fine, but they do need to hang side by side. My work is cyclical and repetitious (like the life of a woman) with small but significant variations that can only be seen when they hang together. I want to show how it is to be a woman. We are full of hopeful expectancy, passive receptivity, empathic activity. Our lives are not linear like men's. We go round and round on the carousel, seeing the same view slightly different every time. Only slightly different. My old friend Michael Salaman from the Slade referred to my paintings as "Pale Quiet Songs", which pleased me very much, for the pale quiet songs are the ones you remember, the ones you keep in your heart.

Elizabeth

Horseshoe and Cocoa

I sit and wait for death, ginger tom on my lap. How I wish there'd been more ginger toms. The moon blesses the bent heads of those dear old Caldey monks. Waiting and remembering. Are they action verbs? Are they even verbs at all? And. If. But. Do they conjunct, preposit? Do they connect?

Mr Smith the caretaker pokes his head round the door. Working late. Seen my light. Cocoa? Yes, please. Like something out of *Harry Potter* he brings a tray of buns – midnight feast – licks the cream right out of one. I wish he'd lick the cream out of this crusty old dusty old tart. To be fucked once more, that's all I ask. When you're old, nobody touches you. You touch things but they don't touch you. The senses go one by one as preparation for the end of age. A cursory hug if you're lucky. A pat on the shoulder. This frail crumbling heap of decay might rub off on you, I suppose.

"Make love to me," I croak. And he does. Lifts me clean off the chair. Ginger tom scarpers. Lays me on my bed. Lifts up my nightdress. Undoes his belt. Shoves his cock in. None of this cootchety-coo crap. We're done in six lunges. I come like a small dry hiccup, he with a short groan, his brace glinting eerily. Then he gets up and goes. He fucked me like I wanted to be fucked. Hard. Fast. Intense. He fucked me like I was still a stunner. He fucked me like I'm still alive.

For the next few nights I leave my light on in the hope of Mr Smith and cocoa. Sometimes I think I dreamed the whole thing. Is dreaming an action verb? If it is then I guess I've lived a full and active life. If waiting and remembering are action verbs I've been busier than most.

Gwen

Mama Pussy

Mère Poussepin should be the most serene of my paintings and yet she is not. I cannot keep her still. She is full of insubordination and giggles. She reminds me of me. As a child I had to take lessons lying on my back for my deportment, but my arms and legs twitched so much Father threatened to tie them up. Oh, Mama Pussy, I can't get you right. Your eyes are too bright, all the better to see you with. Your nose is too long, all the better to sniff you with, and your mouth is saying that under the guise of religion you can do whatever you very well like. You have the exuberance of a flower. The sheer cheek of a raindrop. I can hear you shout aloud at existence. You definitely don't belong on a prayer card.

Moth

Tomorrow

There's surprisingly little to do. I give the bathroom a zesty smile, change the bedsheets, press uniforms for the next two weeks. Prepare lunch at ten thirty. Eat it by ten thirty-five. Cheese sandwich, banana, cup of tea, biscuit. Wonder if she's having fish fingers. Take Freckles for a walk in the land of sniffs and smells. Feel the rain on my face and explain the rain/earth cycle to an imaginary friend. It feels so silent. My hands deep deep in my pockets.

The house is so empty. I do a dance move in the kitchen and feel ridiculous. Stretch out on the sofa, flick the remote. A quiz show, *Inspector Poirot*, *Brief Encounter*. Think about phoning Adam but that train's passed. Maggie? On her way to the States. My father? Deaf, won't answer.

I rearrange the coffee table. That vase. It looks very sterile. I'm a glossy advert for the perfect wife and mother. On the surface.

Calculate that if I walk very slowly I could set off for school at two, which means there's only another hour and a half to get through.

In the end, I leave at quarter to, reach the school at ten past. Another fifty minutes to wait. Luckily Rhys' grandad hops up and we have a little chat about the weather.

"How's the lick lick littlun liking it?"

"Loving it."

"And you? What are you doing?"

"Lots of housework."

He spits his concern at me. "Well, you look after yourself."

"Will do."

Elizabeth

Minnie Again

Minnie puffs up my pillows. Rounder now. Nearly time. Nearly due. "So sorry you lost your friend, Nana. You must be terribly lonely. Wanted to see you one last time before Holly comes. Mum says she'll help and Nick's mother too. I'm so lucky. So I can finish my art degree. Tattoos have become a bit of a strain. Someone came in the other day wanting a devil fellating another devil on his shoulder. 'Oh my,' I said."

What is life after all but one little devil fellating another little devil? A dirty old man in a flasher mac suddenly shocking you. Suddenly popping out at you.

"'Chris'll have to do that for you.' I'm beginning to think the owner of the skin has too much say in the artwork. I want to control my own canvas (not just what goes on it), create my own canvases. Did you see that then? Holly kicked. No stretch marks yet. All those pumpkin seeds did the trick. Big news too. Uncle Ro's engaged at last. Poor old Chiara had so long to wait. And he's on the telly. I'll let you know the channel. Mum's made a breakthrough with the

Seneca Valley virus. We found your old ballerina musical box when we cleared out the attic. Vintage kitsch. So sorry to make it short and sweet. Nick revving up the car as we speak. They'll visit next week. If you can hang on. Love you, Nana."

"Love you too, Cheeks. Always will." Hang on till next week, you stale old fart. Bows scraped out. Let the rains come. Nearly time. Nearly due. (The moon stares unflinching through the window, blessing me, blessing me.)

Gwen

Part of the Painting

Ma Cherie,
Thank you for the hours. Thank you for the moments.
I do not think we shall meet again on this earth.

The rest of his rather short note is unintelligible; his mind and hand have become so shaky. I think I can make out the word 'paint' and 'body', but I cannot be certain. I stick the note to the back of *Girl in Profile* next to the mauve ribbon he gave me. I tried to scratch you out but I still see you. I will always see you. Thank you for the hours. Thank you for the moments. Yes. We live our lives in a succession of moments, and in the end the physical fabric of our bodies will gently dissolve and we shall become invisible. Part of the light. Part of the painting.

Elizabeth

The Objects on my Shelf

Just me in my room then. Just me in my room and the objects on my shelf. Is that what it all comes down to in the end? The nouns on our shelf. The small items left and the feelings we attach to them. That dandelion paperweight we found on honeymoon. I see in it the Eiffel Tower and the concierge with the moustache and the marmalade sandwiches, your execrable "deux big macs, siv vouz play". The snow globe I shake on the perfect world of my children: the science awards, the gym competitions, the piano recitals. The wings I stitched, the wings that flew. Out of reach. The horseshoe we painted silver and hung on the garden gate. It reminds me of the paths I didn't take, the love I didn't make. Strange how when we have love we waste it and when we don't have it it's all we think about, all we crave. A postcard of the *Thinker* and a photograph of me at fifty-three in cap and gown by the statue of Lloyd George. I've got an ear-splitting grin and I'm punching the air. And the ballerina in her box, bent and crouching till the music starts. My life. Pale and quiet. Waiting for the song.

Gwen

Girl in a Mulberry Dress

I don't know where the painting ends and my life starts. Edgar glares at me reproachfully – I have forgotten to feed him again. Gloria brings eggs and milk, scolds me for being too thin. Her small daughter, Thérèse (named after the saint), pitter-patters in the sweet peas. Mulberry dress. Girl in a mulberry dress. What will she turn into? Who will she be? God's little flourish. Rodin's little muse without any arms. Her father, the soldier, was shelled to bits. Augustus and I on the beach near Haverfordwest, collecting cowries in the sand, watching the neophytes plunge into baptism, their selkie heads breaking the sea's caul in rebirth. As I am reborn in his hands. Prometheus. *Mon maître.* Buried with a statue of *The Thinker* in his pocket. His small blue eyes straining to heaven to see if the angels are wearing any knickers. Sometimes I sleep completely al fresco, feel the last dying colours of the earth, the raw siennas, red lakes, cerulean blues, the bolts of silk on a dressmaker's ledge. Turning my colour wheel beyond the pale of the moon. Minerva – goddess of invention. The mystery of the human form in a spatial dimension. I need some more china white from Lefranc if I'm ever to finish *Girl in a Mulberry Dress*. A succession of moments distilled onto canvas. My sketches get smaller and smaller. Let there be light. The size of postage stamps. Counting my rosaries. A dot in infinity. Over and over. Reducing, reducing, ever reducing. Edgar slopes off with the girl in a mulberry dress in the hope of being fed. The callous indifference of children and cats. I rearrange the objects in my room, the flowers and brushes in a jam jar on the barley sugar leg table next to my smock stiff and bleached to china white. My shadow turns grey. Back to Tenby of the Fishes it fled. Cadwallader in his oilskins catching all the little shrimps in his net. All the little shadows.

Moth

Four Weeks Later

No skills, no training, no qualifications, the man in the job centre said. I can balance a soft toy on the end of my nose but that's no good, that won't do. I was Miss Carmarthen at twenty-two but that's no good, that won't do.

What about kids' parties? Get a little van like Drew's. Blow up balloons, make a rabbit appear, disappear. Be a clown. Like God.

I can change a nappy with one hand, a light bulb with the other, but that's no good, that won't do. "Your CV's negligible," the man in the job centre said, "for a woman of thirty-two."

My kids on the other hand have CVs as long as my arm. When they talked, when they walked, when they first did a poop. All because of me. The songs I sang, the hours I dragged, the baths I didn't take, the love I didn't make. All for you.

"It's natural to be anxious," Doctor Morgan said, "when your child starts school. She'll soon get the hang of it. Just continue doing what you do."

Bent and crouching then to their every whim and desire. Bent and crouching under those elemental forces of sun and sea. Is that how it's going to be? Scorched by the sun, submerged by waves, my body found under the white cliffs of Dover, pecked to chips by gulls.

Elizabeth

Adam Again

Ten minutes, the Blue Room, Nurse Tinkerbell shouts. There's to be a talk on Gwen John by renowned artist Adam Shlesinger. My heart flits about with nowhere to hide but death. The older you get the more you come to realise that in the end all narratives twist into one. There is no coincidence. Black and white are tones not colours, he said long ago in an art class in Swansea.

"Elizabeth, your chair awaits." Like frigging Cleopatra. No thanks. I'm deaf remember, and in any case I'm trying to read my book. I don't want to see him grown fat, ugly and old when I'm dying like that poem by Tudor Evans.

"Well, if you change your mind." I won't.

But I do. I can't resist a peep. As the straggling applause fades out and the front door of High View House bangs shut, I stumble over to the window. The truth hits me with a wallop. He's grown old and fat and ugly and I'm dying. But there's still something in his walk, the angle of his head, those hands.

I wrench open the window and shout out of it. "Hey,

Adam, it's me, Moth, remember? You took me to Cardiff Museum, told me about Gwen John and her affair with Rodin. I ran away, wept in a church. It was snowing that day, the children made angels by that statue of Lloyd George." I don't know if I shouted these things or merely thought them, or you were hard of hearing, because you didn't deign to hear me, didn't deign to see me. You simply got in your silver car and drove away, leaving me fluttering at the window. An old woman fluttering at the window. An invisible woman. Is that what we all end up as? Invisible women? Please don't let me be invisible at the end. Please let them see me, let me be seen. Let me see them.

Gwen

My Death

I'll pack a small travelling case and head for the coast. The sea, after all, is still light.

Moth

My So-called Death

Keep away from children, it says on the bottle of pills. Good advice. They'll grow. You'll disappear. You'll be drowned to death. Scorched to death. I'd better get rid of them as a safety precaution, even so. Can't live with 'em, can't live without 'em. They look just like Smarties. I'd better get rid of them. One by one by one.

It goes quickly dark but there's a light in the distance like a beckoning new world. A new death. Shall I head towards it as moths always do?

If I'm to walk I'd better set off by two.

Elizabeth

My Death

Body's packed up, ready for the off. No need for suntan cream or bikini where I'm headed. What word shall I end with? Last word on this earth. Something that'll stick. Love, perhaps.

Tinkerbell swooning over Roan's fine-boned, famous face. "Dear Elizabeth, who'd have thought you were related." Doctor Kharana talking to Dove, his tongue hanging out like Freckles after a bone. Wearing her hair differently in a pretty French plait. Strong as sunlight, deep as the ocean. They flew like arrows somewhere I couldn't follow. And it doesn't matter. I shot my bow as hard as I could. For their sake. Now it's my turn to go somewhere magical. Where they can't follow. Not yet. I take the first step towards the good clear light. Drew fixing up heaven, no doubt, in his white van. This time I shan't turn back.

What word will I end with? Why, mother, of course. No other word needed but mother. Brilliant. Beautiful. Life. My mortal sculptures. My works of art.

I make my way towards the good clean light where I can see and be seen. The new narrative.

Mother. (Job done.)

Zillah Bethell on writing
GIRL IN PROFILE

Why did you choose to write about Gwen John and her experiences in Paris?

I was researching Caravaggio for a short story and a book on Gwen John kept falling out of the library shelf, so I thought: 'Okay, so you want to be written about'. I became intrigued by her passionate relationship with the sculptor Auguste Rodin and her pared back lifestyle in Paris. Her paintings and personal life (on the surface) seemed to contradict each other and I wanted to probe a little deeper.

Why did you choose to title the book after one of Gwen John's paintings – and this painting in particular?

The book is a succession of moments – like pictures. I wanted the writing to be like painting, sometimes glancing, sometimes going in deep... Lots of repetition, symbols taking on a life of their own, semantic resonances.

Gwen John spent most of her career painting women and girls sitting in rooms – often the same woman/girl over and over again with slight alterations – as if trying to explore what it means to be a woman or confronting the process of creating itself.

I saw *Girl in Profile* at the National Museum of Wales which is partly why I used it as the title. I liked the way she left the flaw in the work. It seemed like the perfect title for my own profiles.

What if anything about Gwen John's life inspired the other characters in the book?

I wanted to think of a woman who was the complete opposite of Gwen John, whose whole life was her children, which led me to create Moth. And then, of course, I imagined Moth as an old woman. Waiting in a room. Waiting for her children to visit, the children she had given everything to, sacrificed everything for. Regretting a little, but ultimately rejoicing in that.

Why do you think that women choose to write to death row prisoners, knowing what they have been sentenced for?

I think many women do write out of compassion – there but for the grace of God and all that – but I think your question is hinting that some women write for romantic reasons which is undoubtedly true. I guess a man on death row is the ultimate bad boy and we think we might be able to reform him. Also there would be a great intensity to the relationship, but I suspect the attraction lies in the fact that they are completely unattainable – it is an emotional investment that is risk free. There's no danger of them actually turning up on our doorstep with a bunch of flowers!

How do you see yourself looking back on your life when you are Elizabeth's age?

I hope I'm still writing books. I hope I'm a big part of my happy and successful children's lives and I hope I'm not in an institution of any sort! I don't think I can ask for more. I think I'd be happy with that.

About the Author

Zillah Bethell was born in Papua New Guinea, is a graduate of Wadham College, Oxford and now lives in Tondu, south Wales, with her husband and two young children. She has published two novels for adults as well as several short stories and her upcoming novel for children, *A Whisper of Horses,* will be published in autumn 2016 by Piccadilly Press.

ABOUT HONNO

Honno Welsh Women's Press was set up in 1986 by a group of women who felt strongly that women in Wales needed wider opportunities to see their writing in print and to become involved in the publishing process. Our aim is to develop the writing talents of women in Wales, give them new and exciting opportunities to see their work published and often to give them their first 'break' as a writer. Honno is registered as a community co-operative. Any profit that Honno makes is invested in the publishing programme. Women from Wales and around the world have expressed their support for Honno. Each supporter has a vote at the Annual General Meeting. For more information and to buy our publications, please write to Honno at the address below, or visit our website: www.honno.co.uk

Honno, 14 Creative Units, Aberystwyth Arts Centre
Aberystwyth, Ceredigion SY23 3GL

Honno Friends

We are very grateful for the support of the Honno Friends: Jane Aaron, Annette Ecuyere, Audrey Jones, Gwyneth Tyson Roberts, Beryl Roberts, Jenny Sabine.

For more information on how you can become a Honno Friend, see:
http://www.honno.co.uk/friends.php

BRANCH	DATE
5P	8/16